eveningland

Also by Michael Knight

The Typist
The Holiday Season
Goodnight, Nobody
Divining Rod
Dogfight and Other Stories

eveningland

Stories

MICHAEL KNIGHT

Atlantic Monthly Press
New York

First Grove Atlantic hardcover edition: March 2017

Published simultaneously in Canada
Printed in the United States of America

FIRST EDITION

ISBN 978-0-8021-2597-2
eISBN 978-0-8021-8937-0

Library of Congress Cataloging-in-Publication data is available for this title.

Atlantic Monthly Press
an imprint of Grove Atlantic
154 West 14th Street
New York, NY 10011

Distributed by Publishers Group West

groveatlantic.com

17 18 19 20   10 9 8 7 6 5 4 3 2 1

"It should be quite a sight, the going under
of the evening land. That's us all right.
And I can tell you, my young friend,
it is evening. It is very late."

—Aunt Emily Cutrer to Binx Bolling
in Walker Percy's *The Moviegoer*

contents

water and oil

None of this is true. All of this is true. I want to tell you about a boy in a boat on a nameless creek. About dawn reflected on the water but so dim over the swamp that it failed to illuminate the spaces between the trees.

The boy's name was Henry Rufus Bragg and though he was seventeen years old and would most likely have been offended by my description, there was still enough boy about him that the word remains appropriate. He was handsome but in an unfinished way, especially in summer when the sun freckled his nose and cheeks, blurring his features, a faint constellation half a shade darker than his tan. Six foot three now and not through

I

yet, his bones ached at night with growing pains. A late bloomer, his mother called him, the last of the model airplane builders, a tender boy, a quiet boy, an odd and earnest boy who, like the keeper of some lost art, memorized old knock-knock jokes and repeated them in his head when he was bored.

He lived on the nameless creek with his mother and his father and his younger sister in a white house with long windows and plantation shutters, porches front and back, the only house in sight. The creek drained into Dog River—*La Rivière au Chien* on the original French settlers' maps—and here the boy, called Bragg by everyone who knew him, would nudge the throttle down, boat nosing upward before easing into a plane, spray hissing around the hull, often as not startling a sleeping egret into flight. At moments like those, racing toward the big houses with big wharfs crowding both banks of the river and away from the lush untidiness of the creek, the boy was washed with a feeling he could not have put into words, a kind of rising, something to do with youth and his own fluency behind the wheel and how well he knew and loved this place.

Ten minutes to Dog River Bridge, then forty more between the channel markers in Mobile Bay to Dauphin Island, where the EPA had set up shop. I am writing, of course, about that recent season when the offshore oil rig Deepwater Horizon blew out in the Gulf and the bottom of the ocean sprang a leak. His father owned a marina, where the boy had worked previous summers, scraping barnacles, painting hulls. Though he could have used the boy's help—that summer more than most; he could see the hard times coming—his wife wanted to encourage her son's better instincts and neither of them wanted the children to worry. So they agreed to let him volunteer, after school at first and then, once school let out, from morning until dusk. Because the boy had his own boat, a bearded Oregonian named Jinx MacFee put him to work patrolling the mouth of Mobile Bay, eyes peeled for signs of oil.

Once he'd reported for duty, the boy charted a course back and forth from Fort Gaines to Fort

Morgan, between which Admiral Farragut damned the torpedoes at the tag end of the Civil War. He was careful to steer clear of the hulking tankers headed in and out of port, his wake fading, reconstituting itself, Willie Nelson twanging in his earbuds, summer stoking up with every hour, baseball cap shading his eyes. He chuckled periodically at the jokes he told himself. At noon, he veered in the direction of his father's marina to refill his tank with gas, charge a hamburger at the snack bar, and pass a few minutes in the presence of Dana Pint, the girl I should have known would be the first to break his heart.

In order to entice sport fishermen and leisure craft, the boy's father hired pretty girls to man the snack bar and the bait shop and the gas pumps at his marina. They dressed in white shorts and fitted T-shirts with the marina logo across the breast. It should be noted that the boy had known dozens of these girls over the years, admired their tan legs and their ponytails, highlighted by hours in the sun. They had flirted with him for as long as he could remember, first because he was a child, quick to blush, then because he was tall, good-looking, the owner's son. Dana Pint was different. She was too skinny, for one thing, and her teeth were crooked. Her hair wasn't long enough for a ponytail. Most of the girls wore sneakers to avoid splinters on the dock but Dana Pint went bare-foot, her toes so nimble-looking the boy imagined she could use them to pick up coins.

The first thing she said to the boy that summer was, "What are you looking at?" Like a tough girl in some movie. He'd forgotten not to stare. She was pumping gas for a twin-engine Robalo at the time, one hand on her hip, the boy perched half-way up the steps between the dock and the snack bar. He poked the last of a hamburger in his cheek and walked down to where she stood.

"I'm Bragg."

He extended his hand. She didn't take it.

"I know who you are," she said.

The boy was so unused to hostility, life came so sweetly and easily to him, that he hardly recognized the resistance in her posture and her tone. Any other summer, the dock would have been lined with boats of various sizes, marina girls tending their needs, but on this day, there was only Dana Pint gassing the Robalo, rods craning up from their holders like insect legs, and the boy and his boat, a Boston Whaler skiff, a gift from his father on his fifteenth birthday, tied to a pylon at the end of the dock, stern tailing out into the bay on a receding tide.

"Knock, knock," he said.

"I've got a boyfriend. His name is Pat."

"You're supposed to say *who's there?*"

I asked the boy once about his fondness for knock-knock jokes and he said he liked how they were all the same but different, too, how words and names took on new meanings in the pattern. That may not be an exact quote but it's close. I remember being struck by the ready astuteness of his reply, as if he had wondered the same thing about himself.

Dana Pint squinted at the boy, lips pursed, a mean and wary look.

"You're standing here in this heat telling me a knock-knock joke?"

"That's right. I say *knock, knock*, you say . . ."

"Who's there?"

The boy said, "Orange."

Just then, the gas pump clicked, tank full, and Dana Pint rattled the nozzle back into its slot. For a second or two he believed she was going to let him finish the joke. But she brushed past him and on up the steps to the snack bar, splay-footed, legs so thin he could see inches of daylight between her thighs.

When he wasn't patrolling the bay, the boy could be found in his basement lifting weights, bulking up for the last football season of his high school career—he played tackle on both sides of the ball—or pulling his friends on an inner tube around Dog River, whipping his boat in tight, thrilling, centrifugal turns, the other boys grim-faced, the girls squealing in their bikinis. And sometimes, on Fridays, after he finished his rounds, he'd pass an hour or two with me. For longer than the boy had been alive, I'd lived on a houseboat in the slip I rented at his father's marina. Every Friday, I would buy a six-pack at the snack bar and ice it down and boil whatever crabs I'd pulled up in my traps. The boy's father didn't mind him drinking a single beer in the company of an old man he trusted, his most loyal customer, a widower of nineteen years, living on just enough pension to make rent on the slip. Occasionally, his father even joined us, but most Fridays it was just me and the boy in folding chairs on the aft deck of the *Agnes Rae*—named for my late wife—sipping cold, cold beer and tossing bread ends to seagulls while we waited for the crabs to boil. He was such a polite boy that he indulged my questions about his life without complaint: what exactly was the EPA doing out on Dauphin Island and did he think his team might make the playoffs in the fall and was he making progress with any of those girls he pulled behind his boat? It was in this way that I happened upon his interest in Dana Pint.

"The trashy one?" I said. "The new girl?"

Mornings, I heard her boyfriend's souped-up Nissan whining like mosquitoes on the way to drop her off, saw his lips on her neck in the parking lot, his hands all over, the whole sordid business repeated at five o'clock. When I asked for her help at the marina—let's say I needed a bucket of crickets for my cane pole—she'd huff like working was a nuisance. The only reason she was hired in the first place was the boy's father had offset impending losses with wage cuts and the usual marina girls could no longer afford the job.

The boy said, "I don't think she's trashy."

His eyes were focused on some inward middle distance, his expression exactly as I pictured it as he scanned the water for oil from his boat. You can understand the place he occupied in my imagination. He had so much but remained somehow unsullied by his blessings. It was of no small concern to bear witness as he persevered with Dana Pint.

"Knock, knock," he'd say, when he caught her by herself, and she'd just stare at him like he was simple, though the meanness and mistrust in her eyes began to fade. Once, while Dana Pint was

9

hosing fish guts and sequins of white scales from the fileting station, the boy repeated his usual line and she said, "Goddammit, who's there?"

"Al," he said.

"Al who?"

"Al give you a kiss," the boy said, "if you open this door."

Dana Pint let her mouth gape for a moment.

"How old are you?"

He told her. She shook her head.

"If Pat caught you out here telling me corny jokes, he'd whip your ass."

Then she spritzed him with the hose, a fine, cool mist, before turning the water on her bare feet, which must have been blazing on those hot planks, baked white and warped by the sun.

In those first weeks after the spill, the evening news broadcast endless video shot from helicopters, rainbows of oil on the surface of the Gulf, vast murky swaths of it beneath, and though we understood there was nothing to be gained from rubbernecking our misfortune, we couldn't turn it off, tracking the oil's progress as it drifted from the coast of Louisiana to the coast of Mississippi, ever closer, always closer, the ruined well pumping black gallons of it, black as a bad mood.

The boy aspired to be vigilant, tireless. If oil invaded the bay, he aimed to be the one to spot it. But he worried, some mornings, that by then it would be too late, that it was already too late. Oil would be sucked out of the Gulf and into the bay and into the estuary rivers that fed it, pulled still farther on the tide into the nameless creek, darkening the water like a cloud shadow. On those mornings, he could feel something like panic beating in his veins. He tried to channel his apprehension into watchfulness, his eyes focused on the rolling surface of the bay, the bay iridescent with sunlight, but he could only maintain his concentration for so long before an image of Dana Pint would rise unbidden from the water like a mirage, skinny legs, crooked teeth, sunburned skin peeling on the knobs of her shoulders and the bridge of her nose and the knuckles of her toes. His worry evaporated like bow spray before these visions and no matter how hard he tried to put them out of mind, to focus on the task at hand, he couldn't stop picturing Dana Pint in his boat, smiling at him over her shoulder, pale hair roughed by the wind.

The boy had, with great patience, plied enough information from her to assemble a vague portrait of her life. Nineteen. Junior college dropout. A watcher of television and reader of magazines. She lived with another girl in one half of a duplex. She had no aspirations that he could tell. But she was angry. And she was sad. About what he did not know. The boy was not completely innocent. I'm sure there were other girls willing to submit to his fumblings. He could not have explained the intensity of his attraction to Dana Pint, that blissful ache that welled up in his chest at the sight of her barefooting across the dock, the feeling a distant cousin of nostalgia, as if he'd already won and loved and lost her, but I can tell you he was the kind of boy—as many of us were—drawn to damaged beauty. He wanted, without realizing it, to rescue her. For her part, I suspect, Dana Pint wanted and did not want to be rescued, was both flattered and affronted by the nature of his admiration.

Near the end of May, because there were no other boats in need of fuel just then, she filled the boy's tank for him while he was ordering lunch. Two days later, she let him buy her a hot dog and a Coke but she only ate three bites before dropping the hot dog in the trash and lighting a cigarette. He did not remind her that his father prohibited smoking on the dock.

"No knock-knock jokes today?" she said.

"I was just thinking."

"About what?"

"Maybe you'd like to go for a ride. On my boat."

Dana Pint took a last drag and flipped her cigarette toward the water. It landed short of the edge and the boy watched to be sure the breeze carried it over the side.

"I'm supposed to be working," she said.

"Not right now," he said. "This weekend."

There was a smear of mustard at the corner of her mouth and without thinking, the boy went for it with his thumb but she pulled away, wiped it herself with the heel of her hand, licked the mustard from her skin.

The next day, EPA and Coast Guard men hung long booms across the mouth of the bay as a hedge against the oil, but Jinx the Oregonian told the boy they'd still need him to patrol in case the oil slipped past. The boy made his morning rounds with nausea tugging at his guts, though he'd never been seasick in his life.

At noon, Dana Pint came out to meet him on the dock.

"Knock, knock," he said.

She said, "All right."

He opened his mouth to say *honey bee* but stopped himself just short. Instead, as if she was leading him toward a new kind of punch line, he said, "All right what?"

"Six o'clock," she said. "It won't be so hot out then and we'll still have plenty of daylight. Saturday. You can pick me up right here."

"Honey bee," he said.

Dana Pint did not smile often in the boy's experience. When she did, as now, she pressed her lips together to hide her crooked teeth but the boy had come to recognize the amusement in her eyes, the way they crinkled into black lines, nearly shut, all squint and lashes, like curtains hiding light.

Most nights, the boy built model airplanes in his room. From his ceiling, hung by fishing line, dangled a Spitfire, a Phantom, a Hornet, a Falcon, a Kingfisher, a Dreamliner, a Mustang, a Messerschmitt, a Heinkel, a Fokker, an Airbus, a Foxbat, a Frogfoot, a 747, a Tornado, a Lancer, a Camel, a Nighthawk, a Thunderjet, a Panther, a Lightning, a Tomcat, a Dauntless, a Harrier, and a Concorde, so many planes, he told me once, that their wings ticked together in the breeze sighing through the screen. I'd have guessed the boy would have been more interested in boats but he went on building planes, further evidence that we are enticed by that which is separate from our lives. He had started a P-61 Black Widow but it remained half-finished on his desk, the engine cowling unattached, as if it had landed there for repairs. The boy stretched out in bed, watching the planes sway above him, the air scented with marsh and model glue, his computer linked to an Internet site offering round-the-clock footage of the Deepwater Horizon billowing crude like black smoke into the Gulf.

Rapping at the door—knock, knock.

"Who's there?" said the boy.

His father spilled a puddle of light in from the hall, one hand on the knob, one on the jamb. "Everything all right?"

"Fine."

"Awfully quiet up here."

"Just tired."

His father's eyes flicked to the computer, that ceaseless gush and bubble.

"I'm worried, too," he said.

He was not entirely off the mark. The boy was worried. But not about oil. For hours, he had been fretting over the options for his boat ride with Dana Pint. He considered Middle Bay Light, which was beautiful at sunset. Or they could anchor off of Gaillard Island, where the brown pelicans made their roost, thriving again after near extinction, first because of hunting—their feathers had once been a popular adornment for women's hats—then because of DDT. Now, according to Jinx the Oregonian, the EPA estimated more than ten thousand nests on the island, not just pelicans but herons and skimmers, stilts and terns and rails snugged in among the bulrush. For a while, after his father shut the door and left him, the boy indulged a fantasy in which he pointed his boat due south and kept on motoring into the Gulf until they ran out of gas. He imagined long days waiting for rescue with Dana Pint, nights desperate with stars, the ways they might use their bodies to soothe each other's fear.

He settled, finally, on Fort Morgan Beach. He would pick her up at the marina, skim across the bay in gilded light, trim the outboard and run his boat right up on the sand.

That time of day, there occurred a subtle shifting in the heat, barely noticeable but no less real, like someone had cracked a window on the world, let some fresh air in. Shadows longer on the name-less creek. Dog River still and lovely as a watercolor of itself. Near the mouth of the river was a restau-rant that made the best fried crab claws the boy had ever tasted, better than the marina's—even the boy's father would admit that this was true—and the boy could smell batter on the kitchen exhaust as he cruised under the bridge. A sailboat passed in the opposite direction, close hauled, luffing, three kids in life jackets on the bow. They waved, the boy waved back. He gave the outboard a little gas, his wake a frothy question mark as he curled between the channel markers and back toward his father's marina on the western shore.

Dana Pint was waiting on the dock. He could see her sitting there, silhouetted by the sun. Her bare feet dangled toward the water. He dropped into idle so as not to disturb the few boats in rental slips, mine among them. What he saw next was an optical illusion caused by the angle of the light in his eyes—another head and then another sprouting from hers, torsos, arms, the im-pression weird, mythological. After a moment, he realized that two people were approaching from behind her. Lugging some burden between them, an ice chest. And there came a third body, shorter and rounder than Dana Pint. When he was close enough that the sun was behind the snack bar, he could see more clearly—Dana Pint on the dock and with her, two boys and a girl, all four watching his approach.

"Sorry I'm late," he said.

"You're not late." Dana Pint met his eyes, looked away. "Pat just now pulled up."

Pat was rangy, buzz-cut. Not as big as the boy but big enough. He took the ice chest from his companion and swung one end around for the boy, who accepted it without a word and lowered it into the stern. Pat scowled, flexed his fingers, smoothed his palms over his Jams.

"Heavy," he said.

He hopped into the boat, making it list and wobble, turned and lifted Dana Pint aboard by her waist. She was wearing cutoff jeans and a white T-shirt, her bikini visible through the fabric, the cut and color of it—stringy, black.

"This is Doug," she said. The second boy was helping the second girl into the boat. The girl was too short to make the long step and as she was reaching down with her lead leg, a sandal slipped into the water. The boy reached in quick and grabbed it before it sank. "And this is Kim."

"Pleased to meet you," said the boy.

He shook water from her sandal, handed it over. Instead of putting it back on, she took the other sandal off, tucked both into a straw beach bag. Dark hair, broad cheeks. Almost plump. The roommate.

"Thanks for letting us tag along," she said.

How tiny he must have felt inside his bulk. For a few seconds, Dana Pint kept her eyes on her feet, curled and uncurled her toes. Then she pulled the T-shirt over her head and stared at the boy, shoulders straight, collarbones brittle-looking, her bikini faded and loose over her breasts.

"Let's go," she said.

And so the boy, this decent boy, this harmless boy, shoved off from the dock and set out across the bay, following the route he'd planned for Dana Pint, the boat trailed by hungry, noisy gulls.

Pat rooted in the ice chest, passed around cans of beer.

Kim said, "Is it true that seagulls explode if they eat Alka-Seltzer?"

"It's true," Doug said. "I've seen it."

"Bullshit," Pat said.

Dana Pint sat cross-legged in the bow, the sight of her so close to what the boy had imagined.

"They don't explode." His voice sounded far-away and muffled as if hearing himself through water. "Not the way people think. But the gas bubbles can rupture this thing called a crop. In their throat. It's like a pouch where they store food."

They were all looking at him. He couldn't remember what he'd just said.

Pat laughed and crushed his beer can. "Anybody got an Alka-Seltzer?"

Fort Morgan was situated on a peninsula between the Gulf of Mexico and Mobile Bay. Less than two miles west, on Dauphin Island, stood Fort Gaines. With all those cannons guarding its entrance, the Port of Mobile was believed to be impregnable during the Civil War. And it's true that for years blockade runners hustled in and out under protective fire. Mobile didn't fall until Admiral Farragut got so tired of waiting he abandoned good sense— *Damn the torpedoes! Full speed ahead!* I've studied the historical markers and roamed the musty passageways. An old boardwalk linked fort to beach over acres of bentgrass. You weren't supposed to bring boats up on the shore but the boy did it all the time with his friends. The park service never came around. The fort closed to tourists at five o'clock, warm sand pocked with footprints soon to be erased by tide.

Only once, while Pat and Doug were tossing a Frisbee and Kim was toeing the shallows for sand dollars, did the boy find himself alone with Dana Pint. "Knock, knock," she said from her towel, knee raised, right arm flung over her eyes. The boy's senses were dulled by beer and sun, shame and anger, and he failed to answer straightaway.

"Don't be such a baby," she said. "You know I'm with Pat."

Still the boy did not speak.

"I didn't know he was bringing Doug." She propped up on her elbow, her tone more defensive than remorseful. "I thought maybe you and Kim——"

"Who's there?" he said.

Dana Pint sighed, stood, brushed sand from the backs of her thighs.

"There's something wrong with you."

"There's something wrong with you who?"

He watched her stalk off down the beach, snapping her bikini bottom into place, watched her lead Pat into the dunes and out of sight. He wanted to leave them stranded on the beach. He should have left them. I would have left them. But he was not that kind of boy. Across the bay, paper mills and chemical plants exhaled fingers of blue smoke, beautiful from that distance, like machines for making clouds.

What the boy could not have known was that even as he sprawled there on the beach and even as his party skimmed back over the water and even as he steered the lonely course toward home, oil was stealing into Mobile Bay.

He did not patrol on Sundays. In the morning, he came down to the kitchen in his boxer shorts, fixed a bowl of Raisin Bran without milk—he'd refused milk on his cereal since he was a child—poured a cup of coffee and plopped into a chair at the breakfast table. His mother witnessed all this while talking to his sister on the phone. The boy reached for the paper, which his father had left wedged into a napkin rack. He quartered it, a gesture so exactly like his father that it made his mother smile, and settled his gaze on a section of front page. His face went pale under his freckles. On the phone, his sister, Nan, thirteen, was expounding on the reasons she should be allowed to spend another night with a girl named Esther Agee. The boy shut his eyes a moment, then returned the paper to its place in the napkin rack and left his mother in the kitchen, his cereal and his coffee still untouched, his footsteps heavy on the stairs.

"Hold on a second, Nan," his mother said. She hadn't yet looked at the paper but she did so now, scanning headlines on the front page until she identified the article that had disturbed her son. "Let me call you back," she said.

On the way upstairs, his mother would have mulled potential words of comfort. Something about the resiliency of nature. About how the accidents of men are insignificant by comparison. Such a sensitive boy, her son. But when she pushed open his door, expecting to find him moping in the bed, he was at his desk with the chair turned backward working on a model plane.

"It's not the end of the world," she said, which wasn't at all what she'd intended. His nonchalance derailed her. She sat on the bed, tried again. "By next summer, it'll be like none of this ever happened. You'll see."

He was finally attaching the engine cowling on his P-61 Black Widow. The flight deck and the waterslide still needed paint.

"I'm not worried," he said, and it was true. After Dana Pint's predictable betrayal. After the inevitable headline in the paper. After believing in goodness for no good reason his whole life. In the same way that black is the presence of all colors and nothing, the boy felt so smudged over, he no longer felt a thing.

An estuary acts as a natural filter. Pollutants are washed downstream on currents or inland on the tide and absorbed by marsh plants, canebrake and cattails sopping up impurities through their roots, leaving the water cleansed. On the surface, eventually, the world returns to normal. Only time reveals how it has been changed. So it was with Henry Bragg.

On Monday, he did not report for duty with the EPA. Or on Tuesday. Or on Wednesday. Volunteers came and went so often that Jinx the Oregonian hardly registered his absence. The boy overslept and ate his breakfast and perused the paper, avoiding news of the spill, the failure to cap the well, the potential damage to the bay, the cleanup effort, then retired to his room, the empty days looming before him. I recall that sensation so clearly from my own boyhood. You suppose all those hours will feel like freedom but they don't.

EVENINGLAND

Too many to fill. No satisfaction in them. He
moved around the house in a mysterious and awkward way, as if he had to think about everything
before he did it. I do not mean to give the impression that the boy was nursing his broken heart or
grieving for the water. He was sensitive, yes, perhaps too much so, but he was not a melodramatic
sort. This was something else. He read the first
few chapters of a spy novel but abandoned it on
his nightstand, where it collected rings from lem-
onade glasses. He accepted calls from the girls he
had pulled behind his boat but made no plans. He
finished his P-61 Black Widow but did not hang
it with the rest. It sat on his desk, the paint long
dry. On Thursday, while the boy was in the basement lifting weights, his mother poked her head
into his room looking for laundry and noticed
that the model had been moved. She glanced up
to locate the P-61 among the rest but the planes
were gone, the ceiling returned to its original state
except for a galaxy of eye hooks in the Sheetrock.
His father found them later when he was hauling
out the trash, all those delicate replicas crammed

27

into a black lawn bag too full to fit right in the bin.

The boy heard his parents talking after supper, a low rumble of voices that meant a decision was being made. His father called him out onto the porch.

"You're not volunteering anymore?" he said.

The boy just shrugged. His mother was eavesdropping in the kitchen.

"Why don't you come back to work for me? I could use your help. I had to let the last of the marina girls go this afternoon."

A spark flared in the boy's chest, fizzled before it caught.

"Dana."

"Is that her name?" his father said.

It rained that night, a hard summer rain, swelling the creek and tearing leaves from the trees, but the storm had passed by morning. His father offered him a ride to work but the boy said no thanks, he'd rather take the boat. Liter bottles and wedges of Styrofoam bobbed gently in his wake,

EVENINGLAND

washed by the rain from culverts in town into the watershed, his wake at idle speed little more than white bubbles and swirls that petered out before they reached the shore. The soft burble of the outboard hardened into a buzz as he accelerated into the river, blue swimming pools glittering on every other lawn, those lawns a perfect chemical green. Sometimes, on Fridays, I'd let myself grouse about how the river had been spoiled by becoming fashionable, and though he was too young to remember how it had been, and though he felt vaguely indicted, the boy was always patient with me. This was his river, no matter what an old man said. It looked altered on that morning. He saw no sign of oil, though the creeping possibility of oil was surely part of what he perceived. And it wasn't the big houses or the pools. He hardly noticed those anymore. No one can say exactly what was in the boy's mind as he motored upriver toward his father's marina. But I can guess. He was thinking that everything had been ruined before he was ever born.

✳   ✳   ✳

Except for the heat, it was like winter. Yachts hovered in slips under the seared tin roof but their owners did not come to run them out. The staff had been downsized. Now there was only Willis in the snack bar and Glen in the boatyard. Willis was old and black and Glen was old and white. They didn't like each other. All day they smoked cigarettes in the shade on opposite ends of the marina, the boy moving between them, scraping and painting for Glen when an occasional boat came in needing work, waiting and bussing for Willis when an occasional customer needed food. I knew better than to pester him with questions. Most of the time, he loafed in a chair on the covered deck outside his father's office, thumbing paperbacks and magazines deserted by previous customers. The marina's lending library. Leave one, take one. The boy's father holed up inside, tapping on a calculator and listening to talk radio, window unit leaking condensation down the wall.

The boy was floating on the edge of sleep, a magazine splayed in his lap, when he heard footsteps on the planks. He opened his eyes and there, like she had stepped out of the dream he was about to begin, was Dana Pint.

"I just came for my last check," she said.

The boy blinked and wiped a hand over his face.

"Where's Pat?"

"At work. I borrowed his car."

He lifted the magazine, let it drop onto his thighs.

"I'm helping out around here."

"You got a joke for me?"

"Knock, knock," he said.

"Who's there?"

"Boo."

"I know this one. I go *boo who* and you ask me why I'm crying."

"That's it," he said.

"Not much of a joke."

"I guess not."

"Well," she said, and then she rapped on his father's door and stepped inside, cold air puffing out before she shut the door behind her. A minute later, she emerged with an envelope in her back pocket.

"Have a good summer," she said to the boy and he gave her his most indifferent, his least wounded smile.

That should have been the last time the boy saw Dana Pint, but as she turned to walk away, he pushed to his feet, magazine spilling on the floor.

"Wait," he said.

She stopped and let her chin fall, one hand going to the check in her back pocket like she was worried he might make her give it back.

The boy did not take her out into the bay. Instead, he headed inland, away from the oil, under the bridge and past the houses with their pools. He would cook up a lie to tell his father. Or maybe he'd just tell the truth, suffer the consequences. He didn't care. The mouth of the nameless creek was fringed with sawgrass. Butterflies. Turtles slipping from their logs. The nameless creek was really a dozen creeks, brown rivulets running between islands of swamp. A labyrinth of water. The boy knew the way by heart. He did not take her to his house. He didn't even bother to point it out. He veered deeper into the swamp, the going slower now, cypress branches arching over the creek, painting a filigree of shadow.

Finally, the boy cut the engine, let them drift.

"I hung that rope swing," he said, pointing at the trees. "With my dad. I was ten years old."

The rope dangled from a high and sturdy branch. Three fat knots near the bottom for gaining purchase with your feet.

"Before this boat"—he patted the gunwale—"I used to have a canoe. I'd paddle back here every day in the summer."

Dana Pint swatted a mosquito on her knee.

"Weren't you scared?" she said.

"Of what?"

"I don't know," she said. "Alligators. Snakes."

The boy shook his head.

"They're more afraid of us than we are them."

"Come here," said Dana Pint, and she peeled her T-shirt over her head. He'd expected a bikini top or a bra but there was nothing. Her breasts were small, her nipples the same color as her lips. He kissed her, shoved his hand into her cutoffs. "Hang on," she said, flicking the button with her thumb. She lifted her hips. The boy tugged her shorts over her calves, over her heels. They kissed again. Her mouth savored of ash. He husked his trunks down to his ankles. There was nothing lovely in what they did. She winced and tipped her chin, the tendons straining in her neck.

Then it was done and he hunted up a rag in the console so she could wipe her stomach. They had nothing to say. The sun seemed at a standstill. He ran her back to the marina, his father so engrossed in calculation he'd failed to notice the boy was gone.

His mother was right. This would not be the end of the world. There would be government money coming in, a settlement with the oil company. Jinx the Oregonian roamed the beach shoveling up tar balls like a dog owner behind his pet. Somebody important said the shrimp were safe to eat and we wanted so badly to believe. On the news, we watched cleanup details heaping dispersants on the slicks. Celebrities donated time for Board of Tourism voiceovers. After a while, the sport fishermen started coming back, just the regulars at first, retirees, like me, who didn't care if the amberjack or the mackerel had been swimming in oil so long as they took bait. The boy hustled on the dock, pumping gas, lugging ice, the back of his neck burning in the sun. We did not speak of Dana Pint. In the afternoon, thunderstorms blew in, roaring and cracking for half an hour before breaking apart. The tide rose and fell, rose and fell. In July, they capped the well and the news crews packed their gear.

Spanish explorers sailed into Mobile Bay as early as the sixteenth century. They called it *La Bahía del Espíritu Santo*, Bay of the Holy Spirit. At their approach, the native Muskhogean tribes torched their villages and fled. But it was the French who built the first permanent settlement on the bluffs. Then the British won Mobile in the Seven Years' War, lost it in the Battle of Fort Charlotte. The boy had all of this drilled into him in school.

His football team cranked up two-a-days in August, one practice in the morning, when the field was still wet with dew, and again in the afternoon, when the grass had been scorched crisp by the sun. Running sprints. Hurling his body into tackling dummies, other boys. His coaches praised this new aggression in him, said he could make all-county if he kept it up. Bruises blossomed on his forearms. His shoulders ached at the dinner table but in a satisfying way, like he'd accomplished something real.

On weekends, once again, the boy pulled his friends on an inner tube behind the boat, the lot of them desperate to soak up the summer before it was gone. The river roiled with pleasure craft, ski ropes taut as power lines.

"Knock, knock," said the boy.

"Who's there?" said a girl.

He could see himself mirrored in her shades, his likeness distorted, his hair crazy from the wind. I don't know the punchline. All of this is pure conjecture, the boy's life unspooling while I puttered on my boat, hauling up my crab traps every Friday, icing the beer, light shattering on the bay, clouds racing past like time itself, each of us, every minute, a little closer to the end, not unhappy but nagged sometimes by the unspeakable misgivings of contentment. The boy I knew was already lost as summer edged toward fall, the reflection of his face strange even to him. That's tragic. That's commonplace. It could never have been otherwise. For a second, perhaps, he let himself wonder what had become of Dana Pint, but a girl in splendid sunglasses was waiting for him to finish the joke. I can tell you this: there will be other girls, other disasters. And there will be nights to come, his life mostly behind him, when he will long to hurt like that again.

smash and grab

At the last house on the left, the one with no security system sign staked on the lawn, no dog in
the backyard, Cashdollar elbowed out a pane of
glass in the kitchen door and reached through to
unlock it from the inside. Though he was ninety-
nine percent certain that the house was empty—
he'd watched the owners leave himself—he paused
a moment just across the threshold, listened carefully, heard nothing. Satisfied, he padded through
an archway into the dining room where he found
a chest of silverware and emptied its contents into
the pillowcase he'd brought. He was headed down
the hall, looking for the master bedroom, hoping
that, in the rush to make some New Year's Eve

soiree, the lady of the house had left her jewelry in plain sight, when he saw a flash of white and his head was snapped back on his neck, the bones in his face suddenly aflame. He wobbled, dropped to his knees. Then a girlish grunt and another burst of pain and all he knew was darkness.

He came to with his wrists and ankles bound with duct tape to the arms and legs of a ladder-back chair. His cheeks throbbed. His nose felt huge with ache. Opposite him, in an identical chair, a teenage girl was blowing lightly on the fingers of her left hand. There was a porcelain toilet tank lid, flecked with blood, across her lap. On it was arrayed a cell phone, a pair of cuticle scissors, a bottle of clear polish, cotton balls, and a nail file. The girl glanced up at him now, and he would have sworn she was pleased to find him awake.

"How's your face?" she said.

She was long-limbed, lean but not skinny, wearing a T-shirt with the words *Saint Bridget's Volleyball* across the front in pastel plaids. Her hair was pulled into pigtails. She wore flannel boxers and pink wool socks.

"It hurts like hell." His nostrils were plugged with blood, his voice buzzing like bad wiring in his head.

The girl did a sympathetic wince.

"I thought no one was home," he said.

"I guess you cased the house?" she said. "Is that the word—cased?"

Cashdollar nodded and she gave him a look, like she was sorry for spoiling his plans.

"I'm at boarding school. I just flew in this afternoon."

"I didn't see a light," he said.

"I keep foil over the windows," she said. "I need like total darkness when I sleep. There's weather stripping under the door and everything."

"Have you called the police?"

"Right after I knocked you out. You scared me so bad I practically just shouted my address into the phone and hung up." She giggled a little at herself. "I was afraid you'd wake up and kill me. That's why the tape. I'll call again if they aren't here soon." This last she delivered as if she regretted having to make him wait. She waggled her fingers at him. "I was on my left pinky when I heard the window break."

Cashdollar estimated at least ten minutes for the girl to drag him down the hall and truss him up, which meant that the police would be arriving momentarily. He had robbed houses in seven states, had surprised his share of homeowners, but he'd never once had a run-in with the law. He was too fast on his feet for that, strictly smash and grab, never got greedy, never resorted to violence. Neither, however, had a teenage girl ever bashed him unconscious with a toilet lid and duct-taped him to a chair.

"This boarding school," he said. "They don't send you home for Christmas."

"I do Christmas with my mom," she said.

Cashdollar waited a moment for her to elaborate but she was quiet and he wondered if he hadn't hit on the beginnings of an angle here, wondered if he had time enough to work it. When it was clear that she wasn't going to continue, he prompted her.

"Divorce is hard," he said.

The girl shrugged. "Everybody's divorced."

"So the woman I saw before . . ." He let the words trail off into a question.

"My father's girlfriend," she said. "One of." She rolled her eyes. "My dad—last of the big-time swingers."

"Do you like her?" he said. "Is she nice?"

"I hardly know her. She's a nurse. She works for him." She waved a hand before her face as if swiping at an insect. "I think it's tacky if you want to know the truth."

They were in the dining room, though Cashdollar hadn't bothered to take it in when he was loading up the silverware. He saw crown molding. He saw paintings on the walls, dogs and dead birds done in oils, expensive but without resale value. This was a doctor's house, he thought. It made him angry that he'd misread the presence of the woman, angrier even than the fact that he'd let himself get caught. He was thirty-six years old. That seemed to him just then like a long time to be alive.

"I'm surprised you don't have a date," he said. "Pretty girl like you home alone on New Year's Eve."

He had his doubts about flattery—the girl seemed too sharp for that—but she took his remark in stride.

"Like I said, I just got in today and I'm away at school most of the year. Plus, I spend more time with my mother in California than my father so I don't really know anybody here."

"What's your name?" he said.

The girl hesitated. "I'm not sure I should tell you that."

"I just figured if you told me your name and I told you mine then you'd know somebody here."

"I don't think so," she said.

Cashdollar closed his eyes. He was glad that he wasn't wearing some kind of burglar costume, the black sweat suit, the ski mask. He felt less obvious in street clothes. Tonight he'd chosen a hunter green coat, a navy turtleneck, khaki pants, and boat shoes. He didn't bother wearing gloves. He wasn't so scary-looking this way, he thought, and when he asked the question that was on his mind, it might seem like one regular person asking a favor of another.

43

"Listen, I'm just going to come right out and say this, OK. I'm wondering what are the chances you'd consider letting me go?" The girl opened her mouth but Cashdollar pressed ahead before she could refuse and she settled back into her chair to let him finish. "Because the police will be here soon and I don't want to go to prison and I promise, if you let me, I'll leave the way I came in and vanish from your life forever."

The girl was quiet for a moment, her face patient and composed, as if waiting to be sure he'd said his piece. He could hear the refrigerator humming in the kitchen. A moth plinked against the chandelier over their heads. He wondered if it hadn't slipped in through the broken pane. The girl capped the bottle of nail polish, lifted the toilet lid from her lap without disturbing the contents and set it on the floor beside her chair.

"I'm sorry," she said. "I really am, but you did break into the house and you put my father's silverware in your pillowcase and I'm sure you would have taken other things if I hadn't hit you on the head. If you want, I'll tell the police that you've been very nice, but I don't think it's right for me to let you go."

In spite—or because—of her genial demeanor, Cashdollar was beginning to feel like his heart was on the blink; it felt as thick and rubbery as a hot water bottle in his chest. He held his breath and strained against his bonds, hard enough to hop his chair, once, twice, but the tape held fast. He sat there, panting.

The girl said, "Let me ask you something. Let's say I was asleep or watching TV or whatever and I didn't hear the window break. Let's say you saw me first—what would you have done?"

He didn't have to think about his reply.

"I would have turned around and left the house. I've never hurt anyone in my whole life."

The girl stared at him for a long moment, then dropped her eyes, fanned her fingers, studied her handiwork. She didn't look altogether pleased. To the backs of her hands, she said, "I believe you."

As if to punctuate her sentence, the doorbell rang, followed by four sharp knocks, announcing the arrival of the police.

* * *

While he waited, Cashdollar thought about prison. The possibility of incarceration loomed forever on the periphery of his life but he'd never allowed himself to waste a lot of time considering the specifics. He told himself that at least he wasn't leaving anyone behind, wasn't ruining anyone else's life, though even as he filled his head with reassurances, he understood that they were false and his pulse was roaring in his ears, his lungs constricting. He remembered this one break-in over in Pensacola when some sound he made—a rusty hinge? a creaking floorboard?—startled the owner of the house from sleep. The bedroom was dark and the man couldn't see Cashdollar standing at the door. "Violet?" he said. "Is that you, Vi?" There was such sadness, such longing in his voice that Cashdollar knew Violet was never coming back. He pitied the man, of course, but at the same time he felt as if he were watching him through a window, felt outside the world looking in rather than in the middle of things with the world pressing down around him. The man rolled over, mumbled his way back to sleep, and Cashdollar crept out of the house feeling sorry for himself. He hadn't thought about that man in years. Now he could hear voices in the next room, but he couldn't make out what they were saying. It struck him that they were taking too long and he wondered if this wasn't what people meant when they described time bogging down at desperate moments.

Then the girl rounded the corner into the dining room trailing a pair of uniformed police officers, the first a white guy, straight out of central casting, big and pudgy, his tunic crumpled into his slacks, his belt slung low under his belly, the second, a black woman, small with broad shoulders, her hair twisted into braids under her cap. "My friend"—the girl paused, shot a significant look at Cashdollar—"Patrick, surprised him in the dining room and the burglar hit him with the toilet thingy and taped him up. Patrick, these are Officers Hildebran and Pruitt." She tipped her head right, then left to indicate the man and the woman respectively.

Officer Pruitt circled around behind Cashdollar's chair.

"What was the burglar doing with a toilet lid?"

"That's a mystery," the girl said.

"Why haven't you cut him loose?"

"We didn't know what to do for sure," the girl said. "He didn't seem to be hurt too bad and we didn't want to disturb the crime scene. On TV, they always make a big deal out of leaving everything just so."

"I see," said Officer Pruitt, exactly as if she didn't see at all. "And you did your nails to pass the time?" She pointed at the manicure paraphernalia.

The girl made a goofy, self-deprecating face, all eyebrows and lips, twirled her finger in the air beside her ear.

Officer Hildebran wandered over to the window. Without facing the room, he said, "I'll be completely honest with you, Miss Schnell—"

"Daphne," the girl said, and Cashdollar had the sense that her interjection was meant for him.

Officer Hildebran turned, smiled. "I'll be honest, Daphne, we sometimes recover some of the stolen property but—"

"He didn't take anything," the girl said.

Officer Hildebran raised his eyebrows. "No?"

"He must have panicked," Daphne said.

Cashdollar wondered what had become of his pillowcase, figured it was still in the hall where the girl had ambushed him, hoped the police didn't decide to poke around back there. Officer Pruitt crouched at his knees to take a closer look at the duct tape.

"You all right?" she said.

He nodded, cleared his throat.

"Where'd the tape come from?"

"I don't know," he said. "I was out cold."

"Regardless," Officer Hildebran was saying to Daphne, "unless there's a reliable eyewitness—"

Officer Pruitt sighed. "There is an eyewitness." She raised her eyes, regarded Cashdollar's battered face.

"Oh," Officer Hildebran said. "Right. You think you could pick him out of a line-up?"

"It all happened pretty fast," Cashdollar said.

And so it went, as strange and vivid as a fever dream, their questions, his answers, their questions, Daphne's answers—he supposed that she was not the kind of girl likely to arouse suspicion, not the kind of girl people were inclined to disbelieve—until the police were satisfied, more or less. They seemed placated by the fact that Cashdollar's injuries weren't severe and that nothing had actually been stolen. Officer Pruitt cut the tape with a utility knife and Cashdollar walked them to the door like he was welcome in this house. He invented contact information, assured them that he'd be down in the morning to look at mug shots. He didn't know what had changed Daphne's mind and, watching the police make their way down the sidewalk and out of his life, he didn't care. He shut the door and said, "Is Daphne your real name?" He was just turning to face her when she clubbed him with the toilet lid again.

✻   ✻   ✻

Once more, Cashdollar woke in the ladder-back chair, wrists and ankles bound, but this time Daphne was seated cross-legged on the floor, scrolling on her phone. He saw her as if through a haze, as if looking through a smeary lens, noticed her long neck, the smooth skin on the insides of her thighs.

"Yes," Daphne said, setting her phone aside.

"What?"

"Yes, my name is Daphne."

"Oh," he said.

His skull felt full of sand.

"I'm sorry for conking you again," she said. "I don't know what happened. I mean, it was such a snap decision to lie to the police and then that woman cut the tape and I realized I don't know the first thing about you and I freaked." She clipped her thumbnail between her teeth. "What's your name?" she said.

Cashdollar felt as if he was being lowered back into himself from a great height, gradually remembering how it was to live in his body. Before he was fully aware of what he was saying, he'd given her an honest answer.

Daphne laughed. "I wasn't expecting that. I didn't think anybody named anybody Leonard anymore."

"I'm much older than you."

"You're not so old. What are you, forty?"

"Thirty-six."

Daphne said, "Oops."

"I think I have a concussion," Cashdollar said.

Daphne wrinkled her nose apologetically and pushed to her feet and brushed her hands together. "Be right back," she said. She ducked into the kitchen, returned with a highball glass, which she held under his chin. He smelled Scotch, let her bring it to his mouth. It tasted expensive.

"Better?" Daphne said.

Cashdollar didn't answer. He'd been inclined to feel grateful but hadn't the vaguest idea where this was going now. She sat on the floor and he watched her sip from the glass. She made a retching face, shuddered, regrouped.

"At school one time, I drank two entire bottles of Robitussin cough syrup. I hallucinated that my

Klimt poster was coming to life. It was very sexual. My roommate called the paramedics."

"Is that right?" Cashdollar said.

"My father was in Aruba when it happened," she said. "He was with an AMA rep named Farina Hoyle. I mean, what kind of a name is Farina Hoyle? He left her there and flew all the way back to make sure I was all right."

"That's nice, I guess," Cashdollar said.

Daphne nodded and smiled, half sly, half something else. Cashdollar couldn't put his finger on what he was seeing in her face. "It isn't true," she said. "Farina Hoyle's true. Aruba's true."

"What are you going to do with me?" Cashdollar said.

Daphne peered into the glass.

"I don't know," she said.

They were quiet for a minute. Daphne swirled the whiskey. Cashdollar's back itched and he rubbed it on the chair. When Daphne saw what he was doing, she moved behind the chair to scratch it for him and he tipped forward to give her better access. Her touch raised goosebumps, made his skin jump like horseflesh.

"Are you married?" she said.

He told her, "No."

"Divorced?"

He shook his head. Her hand went still between his shoulder blades. He heard her teeth click on the glass.

"You poor thing," she said. "Haven't you ever been in love?"

"I think you should cut me loose," Cashdollar said.

Daphne came around the chair and sat on his knee, draped her arm over his shoulder.

"How often do you do this? Rob houses, I mean."

"I do it when I need the money," he said.

"When was the last time?" Her face was close enough that he could smell the liquor on her breath.

"A while ago," he said. "Could I have another sip of that?" She helped him with the glass. He felt the Scotch behind his eyes. The truth was he'd done an apartment house just last week, waited at the door for somebody to buzz him up, then broke the locks on the places where no one was home. Just now, however, he didn't see the percentage in the truth. He said, "I only ever do rich people and I give half my take to the Make-a-Wish Foundation."

Daphne socked him in the chest.

"Ha, ha," she said.

"Isn't that what you want to hear?" he said. "Right? You're looking for a reason to let me go?"

"I don't know," she said.

He shrugged. "Who's to say it isn't true?"

"All those Make-a-Wish kids," Daphne said.

She was smiling and he smiled back. He couldn't help liking this girl. He liked that she was smart and that she wasn't too afraid of him. He liked that she had the guts to bullshit the police.

"Ha, ha," he said.

Daphne knocked back the last of the Scotch, then skated her socks over the hardwood floor, headed for the window.

"Do you have a car?" she said, parting the curtains. "I don't see a car."

"I'm around the block," he said.

"What do you drive?"

"Honda Civic."

Daphne raised her eyebrows.

"It's inconspicuous," he said.

She skated back over to his chair and slipped her hand into his pocket and rooted for his keys. Cashdollar flinched. There were only two keys on the ring, his car and his apartment. For some reason, this embarrassed him.

"It really is a Honda," Daphne said.

There was a grandfather clock in the corner, but it had died at half past eight who knew how long ago, and his watch was out of sight beneath the duct tape, and Cashdollar was beginning to worry about the time. He guessed Daphne had been gone for twenty minutes, figured he was safe until after midnight, figured her father and his lady friend would at least ring in the New Year before calling it a night. He put the hour around eleven but he couldn't be sure, and for all he knew, Daphne was out there joyriding in his car and you couldn't tell what might happen at a party on New Year's Eve. Somebody might get angry. Somebody might have too much to drink. Somebody might be so crushed with love they can't wait another minute to get home. He went on thinking like this until he heard what sounded like a garage door rumbling open and his mind went blank and he narrowed the whole of his perception to his ears. For a minute, he heard nothing—he wasn't going to mistake silence for safety a second time—then a door opened in the kitchen and Daphne breezed into the room.

"Took me awhile to find your car," she said.

She had changed clothes for her foray into the world. Now she was wearing an electric blue parka with fur inside the hood and white leggings and knee-high alpine boots.

"What time is it?" he said.

But she passed through without stopping, disappeared into the next room.

"You need to let me go," he said.

When she reappeared, she was carrying a stereo speaker, her back arched under its weight. He watched her into the kitchen. She returned a minute later, empty-handed, breathing hard.

"I should've started small," she said.

He looked at her. "I don't understand."

"It's a good thing you've got a hatchback."

For the next half hour, she shuttled between the house and the garage, bearing valuables each trip, first the rest of the stereo, then the flat screen and the Blu-ray, then his pillowcase of silverware, then an armload of expensive-looking suits and on and on until Cashdollar was certain that his car would hold no more. Still she kept it up. Barbells, golf clubs, a calfskin luggage set. A pair of antique pistols. A dusty classical guitar. With each passing minute, Cashdollar could feel his stomach tightening and it was all he could do to keep his mouth shut, but he had the sense that he should leave her be, that this didn't have anything to do with him. He pictured his little Honda bulging with the accumulated property of another man's life, flashed to his apartment in his mind, unmade bed, lawn chairs in the living room, coffee mug in the sink. He made a point of never holding on to anything anybody else might want to steal. There was not a single thing in his apartment that it would hurt to lose, nothing he couldn't live without. Daphne swung back into the room, looking frazzled, her face glazed with perspiration.

"There." She huffed at a wisp of hair that had fallen across her eyes.

"You're crazy," Cashdollar said.

Daphne dismissed him with a wave.

"You're out of touch," she said. "I'm your average sophomore."

"What'll you tell the cops?"

"I like Stockholm syndrome but I think they're more likely to believe you made me lie under threat of death." She took the parka off, draped it on a chair, lifted the hem of her sweatshirt to wipe her face, exposing her belly, the curve of her ribs, pressed it first against her right eye, then her left as if dabbing tears.

"I'll get the scissors," Daphne said.

She went out again, came back again. The tape fell away like something dead. Cashdollar rubbed his wrists a second, pushed to his feet and they stood there looking at each other. Her eyes, he decided, were the color of a jade pendant he had stolen years ago. That pendant pawned for seven hundred dollars. It flicked through his mind that he could kiss her and that she would let him but he restrained himself. He had no business kissing teenage girls. Then, as if she could read his thoughts, Daphne slapped him across the face. Cashdollar palmed his cheek, blinked the sting away, watched her doing a girlish bob and weave, her thumbs tucked inside her fists.

"Let me have it," she said.

"Quit," he said.

"Wimp," she said. "I dropped you twice."

"I'm gone," he said.

Right then, she socked him on the nose. It wouldn't have hurt so much if she hadn't already hit him with the toilet lid, but as it was, his eyes watered up, his vision filled with tiny sparkles. Without thinking, he balled his hand and punched her in the mouth, not too hard, a reflex, just enough to sit her down, but right away he felt sick at what he'd done. He held his palms out, like he was trying to stop traffic.

"I didn't mean that," he said. "That was an accident. I've never hit a girl. I've never hurt anyone in my life."

Daphne touched her bottom lip, smudging her fingertip with blood.

"This will break his heart," she said.

She smiled at Cashdollar and he could see blood in the spaces between her teeth. The sight of her dizzied him with sadness. He thought how closely linked were love and pain. Daphne extended a hand, limp-wristed, ladylike. Her nails were perfect.

"Now tape me to the chair," she said.

our lady of the roses

Mondays and Thursdays, Hadley Walsh taught art at Our Lady of the Roses School. She was twenty-six years old. She didn't need the money—her father gave her an allowance because he still felt guilty about leaving her mother. She had a black cat named Jezebel. On her days off, she lunched with friends or did some painting of her own, watercolors mostly. Weekends, Hadley dawdled with her boyfriend. This all took place late one winter in Mobile, Alabama.

The school was one story, flat-roofed, brick, nothing much to look at inside or out, but the art room featured a bank of windows overlooking the parking lot and during second and third period, light streamed mercifully through the glass and over the painted cinder block, the scarred supply cabinets, the graphitied wooden stools, the battered sinks. Most of her students were Hispanic or black, only a few white faces mixed in. None of them knew what to make of art class. They seemed to consider it a sort of extra recess, especially the older kids. She had only fifty minutes a week with each grade, K-8, four classes on Monday, five on Thursday, and while Hadley had no illusions about her job, she wanted the students to leave her class knowing at least a little more than they had when they walked in. She had designed projects around the *Mona Lisa* and *Starry Night*, obvious choices. This week they were working on Jackson Pollock, dripping and flicking and spattering paint onto canvases on the floor—an exercise in silliness, the students seemed to think, and that was fine with Hadley, but she had always been intrigued by the way randomness could hint at meaning. Hadley paid for the canvases herself. Our Lady of the Roses didn't have much budget for art supplies.

Her favorite students were the second graders, miniature untarnished versions of their future selves, old enough to be interested and to understand but still young enough that they weren't bound up by self-consciousness and attitude. Third period. Thursday. The sight of them buttoning each other into smocks, men's dress shirts picked up at Goodwill and worn backward over their uniforms, was enough to buoy her through the rest of the day.

Hadley was circling the room, treading carefully between canvases, offering comments and encouragement—"Excellent, Regina. That's it. Don't think too much. Just paint the way you feel"—when Sister Benedicta cleared her throat at the open door.

"May I have a word?"

She tipped her head. Hadley instructed her second graders to keep painting, she'd be right back. The women trailed their shadows into the hall.

"What's up, Sister?"

"I wanted to remind you that this is a Catholic school."

Because of her dark skin and the clipped, slightly foreign inflection in her voice, Hadley had at first believed that Sister Benedicta was Caribbean, maybe from Haiti—the church was always running can drives for Haitian refugees—but the math teacher, Annie Grayson, informed her that Sister had come to Mobile from a convent in Uganda. She'd arrived in November, a replacement for Sister Imogene, who'd been put out to pasture. Sister Benedicta's age was difficult to guess. She might have been thirty-five or fifty. In her clogs, Hadley was a head taller than the nun, but Sister Benedicta was possessed of density. The hallway seemed to tilt in her direction. Hadley had the idea that if you set a marble on the floor it would roll toward Sister's feet no matter where in the building she was standing.

"I'm not sure I follow," Hadley said.

"Shouldn't your students be making art of a more liturgical nature, an Easter project perhaps, something for their parents?"

"They will have something to take home. They'll have these Jackson Pollock canvases. They'll have all the work they've done since Christmas break. They're very proud."

Hung on the wall outside the classroom were the fruits of previous lessons, portraits and Post-impressionist pieces, and Hadley aimed a finger to prove her point. Two doors down, a fifth grader with minidreadlocks burst into the hall, a boy carrying a laminated bathroom pass. At the sight of Sister Benedicta, he reined in his relief at being free of class, his impulse to run or loiter—Hadley could see this struggle playing out in his shoulders and on his face—and forced himself to walk slowly, hands clasped, all the way to the bathroom.

"I'm sure my implication is quite clear," said Sister Benedicta.

Later, drinking shiraz and watching TV at her boyfriend's house, Hadley said, "If creativity comes from God then isn't all art religious?"

She had known Davis Fitch most of her life. Their mothers were friends. Back in kindergarten, she'd had a habit of chewing her ponytail when she was nervous. One day, during recess, with what she recalled as genuine curiosity, no malice at all, he had asked her how it tasted and she allowed him to hold the ends of her hair between his lips for a few seconds before Miss Frederick noticed and shuttled them to the principal's office. In high school, they had avoided the pitfalls of romance by inviting each other to proms and winter formals. Strictly platonic. No pressure, no melodrama. Hadley went off to Brown while Davis stayed in state, but they kept in touch, regular emails, phone calls. They dated other people but nothing serious. After graduation, Hadley spent a lonely year working as a docent in New York and then her parents split and she came home—her mother was a mess—and there was Davis doing wealth management at his father's firm.

"You should ask her that," he said.

He was blond and round-faced, not quite plump. *Soft* was the word Hadley thought sometimes but did not say. Comfortable. He'd hung up his suit and changed into sweatpants, his blue button-down open over a T-shirt, beer bottle in one hand, bare feet crossed at the ankle on the coffee table, the hair on his toe knuckles blond as well. Not long after her return to Mobile, they'd gone out with friends, had too much tequila, ended up in bed. Davis couldn't keep it up. He'd blamed it on the booze but Hadley suspected he was terrified. An awkward few weeks passed before they tried again and then it was nice, tender and thrilling at the same time.

"She doesn't want to hear it," Hadley said. "She's like one of those puffed-up African dictators. Like a female Pol Pot. Worse, she's like one of Pol Pot's toadies. You should see her sucking up to Father Marco. She doesn't care if these kids learn. She just wants them to behave."

Davis massaged her shoulders. He owned the house on Japonica Lane. That's what one did in Mobile—bought a midtown cottage, built equity, got married, moved to a bigger house in Spring Hill. On TV, a female detective poked a dead body with a pencil.

"I think Pol Pot was from Cambodia."

"Whatever," Hadley said.

She'd been surprised at how close to the surface her anger had remained, how quick it was to
flare up now. She had let the rest of her classes
go on with Jackson Pollock, figuring she would
give them a new assignment after Mardi Gras
break, something more to Sister Benedicta's liking, but all afternoon her heart had raced and her
eyes were hot, and she left the art room a disaster,
paint everywhere, smocks in a heap, brushes un-
washed. She didn't usually spend weeknights with
Davis—her mother insisted that she keep her own
apartment—but she hadn't wanted to be alone.

She was hunting boxers to sleep in when she
found it, a black velvet ring box hidden among the
socks in Davis's top drawer.

Contrary to popular belief, Mardi Gras started in
Mobile, Alabama. In Mobile, not New Orleans.
The first masked ball took place in 1704, the first
parade in 1711, a dash of revelry before Lent.
Schools are closed during the last week of the sea-
son, so Hadley was released from Sister Benedicta.

On Saturday, she arrayed herself in satin and attended the Mystics of Time Ball with Davis, the ring box snagged like a hangnail in her thoughts.

On Sunday, she had dinner with her father, Louis, and his new wife, Pam, a physical therapist. They'd met after surgery on his rotator cuff. After dinner, he presented Hadley with three hundred dollars cash. "Fun money," he called it, holding her car door open. "Next time bring your young man."

On Monday, she went out for beer and oysters with her friends. Only Peyton was married. The others had been her bridesmaids. Now Peyton was pregnant, beaming, sipping Diet Sprite and nibbling saltines. She told stories of her husband's befuddlement—with birthing class, crib assembly, pregnancy sex. The others howled, their beauty not just physical but in the way they occupied space like no one else was in the room. Peyton volunteered, belonged to clubs. Virginia and Caroline both worked part-time at a funny little store on Old Shell Road where a certain kind of woman could find certain kinds of clothes and certain kinds of accessories. They were waiting for their real lives to begin. They had seemed so proud of Hadley when she went off to school and they seemed pleased to have her home, back in the fold, but she had detected—or thought she had detected—a hint of gloating in their welcome as if they'd known all along she would return, nothing accomplished. She didn't tell them what she had found in Davis's sock drawer.

Hadley was invited to a party on Fat Tuesday, king cake and champagne in a downtown loft, the final parade of Mardi Gras fizzing past below the balcony. The party was hosted by Marlowe Boggs, a lesbian, somewhere in her fifties, with a shock of dyed black hair and a lover half her age. Marlowe owned a gallery on Bienville Square. She'd sold a few pieces for Hadley: a lighthouse at sunset, an antebellum manse. Tourists liked that sort of thing. Weeks before, Hadley had asked Davis to come along but his presence at the party left her ill at ease. He roamed the loft like a country politician, shaking hands, admiring the exposed brick and the paintings on the walls, trying too hard. "He's like a golden retriever," Marlowe said.

When the parade cornered onto Royal, Davis grabbed Hadley's hand and hustled her out onto the balcony. Down below, the sidewalk on both sides of the street was five, six deep with unruly humans, their shouts and catcalls misting in the chill. On the emblem float, a jester chased a skeleton around a broken pillar, Folly chasing Death.

They were the first to leave the party. Hadley claimed that she was tired. In Davis's bed, she pinned his wrists and rolled her hips and shut her eyes. Afterward, she dreamed of Sister Benedicta holding a red umbrella in the rain.

In the morning, according to plan, Hadley met her mother for brunch at a restaurant famous for crabmeat omelettes. Her mother was wearing church clothes, pearls, her forehead crossed with ash.

"You didn't go to Mass?" she said.

"I forgot."

"That can't be true."

"I didn't think about it."

Her mother's eyelids drooped in disbelief but Hadley was being honest. She'd scribbled a note while Davis was still asleep, hopped the bus to her apartment to feed the cat, shower, brace herself for these hours with her mother, never once considering the obligation of Ash Wednesday. Before leaving, she'd picked Jezebel up, kissed her between the eyes and set her on the mat outside the door. Jezebel did a mewling whine. The complex was gated and walled. Lots of pets from the apartments prowled the grounds during the day, but Jezebel preferred the climate-controlled interior, preferred her perch on the back of the couch. "Think of it this way," Hadley had said, "at least you're not having brunch with my mother." Now here she was, at a two-top by the window, trying not to wither under the chilly skepticism of her mother's gaze.

"There's a two o'clock at Saint Ignatius," her mother said.

"Do we have to do this, Mona?"

Since his remarriage, Hadley's father had insisted that she address him by his first name—he didn't want to be Dad and Pam; he wanted Hadley to put him on the same footing as his new wife—and this usage had bled over into her relationship with her mother. It had the added advantage of driving her mother crazy. She glared at Hadley over her iced tea, a lemon wedge bobbing near her lips, the ash smudged and dirty-looking on her brow.

"You can call your father and that woman whatever you like but I'm your mother and I am not on a first-name basis with my child."

The waiter arrived and listed the specials but Hadley didn't hear. She was thinking about the ring box. She'd fished it out the night before while Davis was brushing his teeth but she couldn't bring herself to look inside.

"Take that hair out of your mouth," her mother said, when the waiter was out of earshot. "I thought we'd broken you of that a hundred years ago."

Hadley hadn't noticed what she was doing. She tongued the ends of her ponytail before slipping it from her mouth. It tasted like stale bread.

"Have you seen him?" her mother said.

"Louis? We had dinner last weekend."

"And?"

"And what?"

"And how is he? Is he happy?"

After brunch, Hadley drove to the Jesuit college up the road, sketchbook on the passenger seat. She didn't go to Mass but she wanted to make some pencil drawings of the chapel. Perhaps she would paint it tomorrow, a kind of penance for the way she'd treated her mother. It was warm for February, hushed, pleasant beneath the pines.

She sketched through one Mass and into the next, the first crowd pouring out onto the steps, the parking lot emptying and filling up again, another crowd, nearly identical to the first, entering the chapel. She worked quickly, as she always did with preliminary sketches, trying different angles, now focusing on the steeple, now on the gothic accents around the double doors, but the steeple looked like a steeple, the doors like double doors, nothing revealed beyond their simplest incarnations. She was just closing her sketchbook, dissatisfied with her efforts, when Mass let out and she spotted Sister Benedicta in the crowd. At school, the nun wore an unflattering calf-length black skirt and short-sleeved blouse with her wimple, but today she was outfitted in full habit. She stood at the top of the steps, blinking in the sun. It would have been easy enough for Hadley to slip off to her car and drive away unseen but even as she was trying to make up her mind, Sister Benedicta saw her. She hiked her skirt, revealing white athletic socks, and headed in Hadley's direction over the lawn, her eyes brushing Hadley's unmarked brow, pinning her in place.

"Miss Walsh."

"Hello, Sister. You don't go to Mass at Our Lady?"

"I generally do, yes, but this morning I was asked to pray with a sick parishioner. This Mass suited my schedule."

Hadley hugged the sketchbook against her chest.

"I've been drawing the chapel."

"Inspiration for a new art project?"

Shadows wavered on the grass.

"Could I buy you a cup of coffee?" Hadley said.

To her surprise, Sister Benedicta agreed. They took Hadley's car. Hadley had to clear the floor on the passenger side of fast-food wrappers, unopened mail. Sister Benedicta looked out of place in the coffee shop but she would have looked out of place most anywhere in that habit. Hadley wasn't sure what she'd hoped to accomplish by her invitation, perhaps only to prove to herself that she would not be cowed. She didn't know what to say. They passed a few minutes with small talk. Yes, Hadley had grown up in Mobile. Yes, she'd enjoyed her time in Providence. Yes, she supposed she was glad to be home. She was tempted to tell Sister about her dream, the image of the nun holding a red umbrella in the rain. She wanted to say something outrageous, to put Sister Benedicta on her heels. She had an impulse to tell her about the ring box but tamped it down.

"So, I'm sorry, I'm sure you get this all the time," Hadley said, "but I can't help wondering why you decided to become a nun."

Sister Benedicta said, "I was called."

"That's what they all say."

"Because it's true."

"Well, then, how were you called? Did you hear God's voice? Did you have a vision?"

Sister Benedicta sipped her latte, holding the mug with both hands, leaving a smear of foam on her top lip. She set the mug on the table and looked at Hadley.

"I was a girl, fourteen years old. There was a convent school in our town. The nuns were kind. They were like strange birds. One night, soldiers broke into our house looking for my father. They raped my sister first. As they were raping me, I prayed that if I survived and if He would have me, I would marry myself to the Lord. At that moment, He lifted me out of my body. I felt no more pain, just warmth, release."

Her gaze never left Hadley's face, her voice never wavered. The man at the next table was staring around his newspaper.

"Jesus," Hadley said.

"Indeed."

Davis phoned that night. He wanted to come over but Hadley told him she needed quiet time. If he was disappointed, he didn't let on. She could hear the TV playing in the background.

"What are you watching?"

"I don't know," he said. "Some movie."

Jezebel purred in her lap. She was inevitably hungry for affection when Hadley let her in at night.

"What channel?"

He told her and Hadley turned the TV on and found the channel he was watching. She'd seen this movie before.

"I meant to ask," Davis said, "what did you give up for Lent?"

"I'm still thinking about it," she lied, and then she was telling him about her day, the story spilling out in a rush, how she'd run into Sister Benedicta by chance outside the chapel, the coffee shop, her stupid question, Sister Benedicta's reply.

"Jesus."

"That's what I said. And I know it's terrible, I know it is, I can't even begin to imagine something like that, but I swear she took pleasure in telling me. It was creepy. Like it gave her power. I felt like she'd slapped my face. How wicked am I for thinking that?"

"On a scale of one to ten? About an eight."

"What did you give up for Lent?"

"Doritos," Davis said.

Jezebel sprang up suddenly from Hadley's lap and darted into the kitchen, skittering under the table and out the other side, pursuing nothing.

Back in high school, Hadley had applied to Brown, along with Duke and Yale and Stanford and Columbia, because those schools had first-rate art programs and she was an excellent student and her teachers had encouraged her and none of those schools were less than five hundred miles from Mobile. She wanted to meet new people, have an adventure, experience something all her own. She wasn't thinking about her future, not really, and when she did, it took on the hazy contours of a half-remembered dream, a vision, she believed, that would come into focus eventually without much effort on her part. She'd gone to Brown because it was the only one of those places that had accepted her, a detail that hadn't bothered her at the time. She'd chalked it up to fate. And Hadley had loved Providence in some ways—how the leaves came alive in their dying every fall and how the old brick dorms gave her dreams of upright New England ghosts—though it never felt like home. She hadn't exactly fit in among her classmates with their ambitious piercings and aggressive tattoos. They were serious about their art, pretentious in the way that only undergraduates can be pretentious, even if they weren't always very good. They seemed to know something about the world that still eluded Hadley. Hadley had never met so many actual homosexuals and one night, she let a girl named Tori Samples kiss her breasts before bursting into laughter at the thought of what she was doing. Tori was incensed. "You need to let go," she'd said, glowering beneath a row of eyebrow rings, and Hadley had thought, Let go of what?

It was also up in Providence that Hadley had stopped attending Mass. There had been a scandal involving a parish priest and three young boys, the requisite cover-up, editorials in the paper, angry protests, but even Hadley realized in some vague way that she was just using the scandal as an excuse. The truth was she didn't believe in a God who demanded her adoration. She believed in mystery. She believed in patterns and signs. She believed that quantum physics and the theory of relativity could not coexist in the same universe without help. She believed that there was no evolutionary reason for the way beautiful things could take the breath away or for the power of Art with a capital A. She missed the ritual of the Mass sometimes, the way it emptied her mind like meditation, but she could conjure that same powerful emptiness staring at the blazing WaterFire sculpture over the rivers in downtown Providence or while painting or in a sailboat on Mobile Bay.

On impulse, however, the Sunday after Mardi Gras, she drove to Mass at Our Lady of the Roses. The church was small and old, listing toward shabby, but charming for those reasons, the flaking paint and plaster, the tired kneelers, though Hadley understood that the parishioners probably did not find those details quaint. The only other white faces she saw were elderly women, most likely women who had lived in this parish before it had gone to seed. She recognized several students from her classes. One of her second-grade girls, Regina, came over in her pink dress to give Hadley a hug. Sister Benedicta was sitting in the front row. Perhaps it was Sister Benedicta's presence or because she had stayed away too long, but Hadley couldn't give herself up to the proceedings. She had trouble paying attention to the Gospel and the homily and she couldn't remember when to kneel and parts of the Nicene Creed escaped her.

All of which is why it came as such a surprise when inspiration struck. The priest was blessing the Host before Communion. Behind the altar was a stained glass window depicting a rose, a symbol of Mary. Light beamed thickly, dustily through the window and she could see bird shadows playing on the glass, swooping and darting and disappearing into nothing. At that moment, in that light, the braces between the panes were cast in high relief and Hadley was acutely conscious that the flower was composed of dozens of smaller pieces of glass, rather than of a single piece. The word *mosaic* passed through her mind and then the word *collage* and she thought, Yes, that's it, of course, we'll do collage. The lesson fell into place as she lined up for Communion. The students would collage a rose. Picasso and Matisse had both worked in collage. The symbolism of the rose would please Sister Benedicta but it wasn't so overt that it made Hadley feel like she was caving in. After she had her sip of wine—*The Blood of Christ. Amen*—Hadley hurried out into the day without waiting for the closing prayer and hymn.

That afternoon, she put almost four hundred dollars on her Amex—her father paid the bill— loading up on construction paper and poster board. She bought dozens and dozens of magazines for cutting up and bolts of colorful felt so the students might employ different textures. She bought thirty pairs of scissors just in case. She bought gallons of glue. Her last stop was Walmart and as she was pushing her cart away from the store, looking for her car, she noticed a new message on her cell. Her father. For a second, she thought maybe he'd been contacted by the Amex people about all the sudden charges but the card was in her name, even if the bill went to his address. In the middle of the parking lot, still not sure where she'd left her car, she thumbed in the voice-mail code and pressed the phone against her ear.

"Hey, sweetheart, it's me, it's Dad, it's Louis. Listen, I just had the most intriguing call from your young man. He wants to buy me lunch next week. He wants to talk man-to-man. It's all very hush-hush. He swore me to secrecy but I wanted to talk to you before we meet. I think I know what this is about. I hadn't realized you two were so serious. Anyway, give me a shout when you have a minute. Pam says hello."

As his words washed over her, the tips of her fingers began to tingle and Hadley worried she might drop the phone. She could picture the scene so clearly, Davis and her father in some dim restaurant, Davis asking her father for permission to propose, for his blessing. A car horn honked behind her and Hadley realized she was blocking an open spot with her cart. She slipped the phone into her purse and resumed her search, rolling past her own car twice before she recognized it.

Davis played soccer in the park with friends on Sunday afternoons. Hadley drove directly to his house, her trunk stuffed with art supplies. She had a key. She let herself in through the kitchen door and stood there for a moment on the tile, a breakfast plate drying in the dish rack, her own face smiling at her from a photograph magneted to the refrigerator. Taken last year, a weekend at Gulf Shores. As she moved from kitchen to living room to bedroom, the house felt stuffy and too neat, not a single stray sock on the floor, no half-empty glasses sweating on end tables. Hadley wasn't sure what she intended but it didn't matter. The ring box wasn't there. She rummaged through his boxers and socks, poked her fingers into corners. Nothing. She checked the other drawers to be sure. The curtains were drawn, light seeping in around the edges.

Back at her apartment complex, Hadley was met by a commotion in the parking lot. Several of her neighbors were gathered around a woman Hadley recognized but couldn't name—red hair, freckles. She had a little boy, Hadley thought, but she didn't know his name either. More neighbors peering down from the gangways on several floors. Hadley wanted to slip by unobserved but a voice called out to her. She stopped, arms laden with shopping bags. The crowd parted. The woman with red hair and freckles was crying.

"I'm so sorry," she said. "I didn't see her."

At the woman's feet was a dark crumple the size of a loaf of bread. Wet-looking. Furred. Hadley didn't know what she was seeing and then she did. She lugged the art supplies to her apartment on the second floor, dropped them in the foyer, fetched a garbage bag from the box under her kitchen sink. Back down the stairs, feeling watched, feeling blurry and slow.

"I'm sorry," the woman said again. "She didn't suffer."

She reached for Hadley but Hadley flinched and the woman withdrew her hand. Someone else said, "It was an accident. I saw it. Your cat just ran right out in front of the car."

Hadley tugged the garbage bag inside out and used it like a glove to pick up the body so she wouldn't have to touch it, then let Jezebel's weight, as the cat sagged to the bottom, turn the bag right side in. There was a Dumpster in the far corner of the lot. Hadley weaved between the cars, flipped the bag over the lip and returned to her apartment, fixing the chain behind her. The phone rang but she didn't answer. A few hours later, it started ringing again. She was busy. She was faraway. She was cutting shapes from felt and glossy magazines to teach her students about collage.

The lesson did not go as she had planned. Somehow her students failed to grasp what Hadley had always considered a fairly simple and liberating concept. She thought perhaps Picasso and Matisse had been the wrong examples, though she had wanted to allow her students the freedom to go abstract if so inspired. Even the rose Hadley cobbled together on the fly from scraps and pieces, a literal rose with recognizable petals and stem, had failed to get the point across. "Real rose petals aren't uniformly red," she said. "There are lots of different shades in them, even blacks and browns, and when you see the rose in a garden it's tinted with shadow and light which brings more colors into play, and the petals don't have the same texture as the stems. You can use the pieces you've cut up to capture those different shades and textures." She roamed between the long tables, holding her quick collage up for display. Rain wisped against the windows. One of her eighth graders, Dante, was playing a video game on his phone.

"Pay attention, please, Dante. This can be fun."

"I'm finished."

She gave him her best skeptical teacher look. He pushed his square of poster board over for Hadley to see. On it, he'd glued an ad for lunch meat, ham slices on a cutting board, torn intact from the pages of a magazine.

"What's this supposed to be?"

"The Last Supper," Dante said.

Even her second graders didn't understand, but by then, just third period, Hadley was exhausted from the effort of explaining and she let them proceed however they liked, clipping and pasting images of fashion models and movie stars and vistas from travel magazines of places they would most likely never see. She paused at Regina's stool.

"Very nice," she said, not really looking.

Her attention was focused on the scene outside the windows—Sister Benedicta haranguing a deliveryman in the parking lot. In her left hand, she held a red umbrella. Rain slicked on the pavement. Hadley's skin prickled. Regina was saying something.

"What's that?"

"I asked what you gave up for Lent, Miss Walsh. I gave up being mean to my little brother."

"I gave up giving things up," Hadley said.

Hadley didn't think she could bear the teacher's lounge over lunch so when the bell rang, she trotted through the rain to her car and shut herself inside, ponytail dripping down her back. It only took a minute for her breath to fog the windshield. She checked her phone. A text from Davis.

miss you tried to call need to talk

Hadley tucked the end of her ponytail between her lips and let her head tip forward until it was resting on the steering wheel. She sucked rainwater from her hair. She closed her eyes. She wanted to pray but she couldn't make her mind go quiet. Words flickered in her head like the mixed-up letters in a Jumble—*ring, art, rape, ash, nun, cat, collage*—and she had the sense that if she managed to organize them into coherence she might recognize some hidden meaning, some grand design. After a while, there came a rapping at the window. Hadley lifted her head and spit the ponytail from her mouth. Sister Benedicta loomed in the rain, red umbrella vivid as a rose.

"Lunch period has been over for half an hour." She knocked again, harder this time. "Your students are wondering where you are." She tried the door handle. Hadley couldn't remember locking it but she must have. "Are you all right, Miss Walsh? Your students are worried."

Hadley punched the key into the ignition and cranked the engine. Sister Benedicta lurched away from the car, startled. Her lips were moving but her voice was lost in the rain.

Hadley merged onto I-10, headed east, no particular destination in mind, hardly noticing the billboards flashing by above her, the other cars. On her left, downtown Mobile emerged against the rain, those old hotels and bank towers somehow flat and unreal, like images in a photograph. Across the interstate sprawled the state docks and the shipyards, tankers and barges on the river, the river pocked by rain. There was a game kids had played when Hadley was a girl. You tried to hold your breath all the way through the George

Wallace Tunnel. And as the interstate sloped beneath the river and the city disappeared, Hadley
inhaled deep and kept it in. She could hear her
pulse all of a sudden, could feel the weight of
the river, the pressure of it in her ears. The road
sloped down and gently down, her heart pounding behind her ribs, and then gradually back up
again, and in the distance, past the red taillights
of the cars ahead of her, the mouth of the tunnel
wavered into view, round and gray and small as a
dime. She imagined herself in the backseat of the
family wagon, her mother's hairdo, the stubble on
her father's neck. There had been no reward back
then for holding your breath all the way through,
just the vaguely grown-up pleasure of accomplish-
ment. The exit swelled to the size of a quarter, the
rim of a wine glass, the lid of a pot and Hadley
was put in mind of those near-death experience
stories you heard sometimes, the light at the end
of the tunnel. There was a scientific reason the stories were all the same. She knew that, though she
couldn't remember what it was. She also knew that
you had to return to this life to speak of the other

side. Her chest was tight, her throat constricted. Hadley clenched her teeth and stepped on the gas and the car burst out into the day. For a blurry second, before the wipers cleared the windshield, the rain obscured her view, but then like magic, like a miracle, the world came back into focus—a stretch of bridge over the silver expanse of Mobile Bay—and she exhaled.

jubilee

These two, satisfied towns gaze at each other like
old flames across Mobile Bay—handsome, hide-
bound Mobile with its lawyers and its cemeteries
and blithe Fairhope, pretty Fairhope, with its gal-
leries and boutiques, Point Clear draped along the
eastern shore like a string of pearls. Used to be, the
right kind of Mobile family escaped to Fairhope
in summer for the breezes, fleeing the humidity
and mosquitoes and the bad air from the mills.
The air is better now but some of those families
decided to stay—why shouldn't life be sweet as
summer all year round?—enrolling their children
in the little private school, wives fondling tomatoes at the farmer's market, husbands shuttling

half an hour back across the bay during the week, that original migration in reverse, past the seafood dives and bait shops and the decommissioned battleship moored for tourists, to offices in downtown Mobile.

Such is the case with Dean and Kendra Walker. Here is Kendra in the kitchen, slicing hearts of palm while Dean prepares the grill out on the wharf. Friday, late September. One has the impression that these long evenings will last forever, but already night is settling in by seven thirty and it's cool enough that Kendra will drape a cardigan over her shoulders when she goes out. While he waits for his wife to join him, Dean drinks single malt and pitches a tennis ball into the bay for their yellow lab, Popcorn, to retrieve.

From where she stands, Kendra can look out over the great room and through the windows along the porch. The lawn with its Bermuda grass and mossy live oaks. Then the boardwalk and the seawall and the beach, nearly covered at high tide. A row of wharves reaches into the bay, all those hammocks and Adirondack chairs, all those white boats suspended on their lifts. Across the water, a blazing sunset, that marvelous cliché.

The windows are open. Insects rattle in the grass. She scrapes the hearts of palm from the cutting board into a wooden bowl with black olives and endive. She'll wait to toss the salad until the steaks are nearly done. Her hands are bare, rings waiting on the sill. Their son, Thomas, named for Kendra's father, is back at school, a sophomore at the University of Alabama. The past month has been quiet. Kendra washes her hands, replaces her rings.

She's outside and across the boardwalk when Popcorn comes bounding down the wharf to greet her. He knows better than to jump on Kendra so he hops and wags, careful not to make contact, and she palms his back to settle him, his fur damp, his smell brackish. "Easy boy," she says, and off he goes, paws thudding on the wood, to let Dean know that she's coming.

And here is Dean in weekend attire—worn polo, white shorts, brown loafers. His ankles are bare. His shins retain the faint patina of his summer tan. He will be fifty in November. Kendra has already picked out the invitations to his party. He does not look his age. He plays tennis twice a week. He has the posture of a military man, though he never served. He is taller than he appears. It's his eyes, she thinks. The gentleness in his eyes belies his height.

She takes her place at the wrought-iron table. Dean fixes her a drink. They talk of nothing for a while—his day at work, hers at home—the conversation more rhythm than exchange of information. Music drifts over from the old hotel. Must be a band on the patio tonight. This silver bay is as familiar to Kendra as her husband's voice but still a mystery, the only place in the world where shrimp and crab and flounder occasionally abandon deep water in the summer and swarm the shallows for no good reason, practically leaping into nets and buckets, presenting themselves for a feast. Jubilee, they call it, voices ringing along the shore. There was no jubilee this season but nobody around here seems particularly concerned, least of all Dean and Kendra. They have the sunset and music from the old hotel. They have twenty-two years of marriage. They have good Scotch and a good dog and not a cloud in sight.

Popcorn drops a waterlogged tennis ball at Dean's feet and he launches it as far as he can without rising from his chair. Before it hits the water, Popcorn is sprinting for the edge of the wharf, hurling his body elongate into the air. Even at high tide, it's a three foot plunge and watching the dog make his leap never fails to impress Kendra, the sheer unafraid athleticism of it. Once Popcorn retrieves the ball he'll have to swim it all the way back to the beach, then run it all the way back out to the end of the wharf where he will drop it at her husband's feet again. Dean stands and wipes his right hand, his throwing hand, on the seat of his shorts.

"Well," he says, "let's light this fire."

In preparation for the moment, he has already stacked the charcoal and rinsed it with lighter fluid and rolled the grill out from under the tin roof. Popcorn returns with his tennis ball, so Dean chucks it one more time into the bay before striking a match and touching it to the coals, drawing his fingers back quickly to avoid the flame.

September flares out with a heat wave. There is work to be done around the house. There is always, it seems to Dean, work to be done. Sometimes he imagines that his wife begins redecorating in one corner and works her way month by month, room by room until the whole house has been remade and she can begin again. He doesn't ask questions. He compliments the changes when he notices them. This house has been in his family for three generations but it is wholly Kendra's now.

Scaffolding goes up. Blue tarps. Trucks in the morning when Dean is leaving for work. Hammers and shouts. The housekeeper, Rosie, complains that workmen are always underfoot. Popcorn hides under the bed. Hispanic painters in spattered white, hardly more than boys, appear on the doorstep and ask if they might drink from the hose. Then, like shelling a shrimp, the scaffolding comes down, tarps are removed. Glistening, the Walkers' house emerges. One night, Dean pulls into the driveway and it is as if they have razed the original and constructed an exact replica in its place.

"Everything looks great," he tells his wife. "Just really great."

They are sipping Scotch in heavy glasses, a fire in the hearth, though it's far too soon. Kendra drove past a farmer selling wood from the back of his truck. She was inspired. Dean thumbs the thermostat way down so they can enjoy it. On TV, the same old news. They will elect a president in November, less than a week before Dean's birthday.

"I was at the caterer's today."

"Hmmm."

Dean can feel himself drifting off.

"We'll have the tenderloin for sure," Kendra says. "And oysters, fried and raw. They're suggesting chicken, too, but I was thinking catfish. Or tuna. Which would you prefer?"

"That sounds perfect."

She nudges him with her elbow.

"I asked you a question."

"I'm sorry," he says, rubbing his face. "Ask me again."

"Do you even care about this party?"

He can hear something close to exasperation in her voice, more emotion than the subject warrants, but he lets it be, figures it will smolder out on its own. Dean votes Republican without fail but he suspects that Kendra is leaning Democrat this year. Her ballot history is inconsistent. She voted for Clinton in '92, then against him after he cheated on his wife. She voted for Bush both times, then for Obama. Dean can't suss out the pattern but her private logic moves him. The fire twitches and sags. Popcorn sprawls before the flames until the heat becomes uncomfortable, then, sighing, retreats to the kitchen where the tile is always cool.

"Is that what you asked me before?" Dean rests his head on her shoulder. "I swear I heard something about catfish."

"Don't tease," she says. "I'm not in the mood."

Ten more minutes pass before Kendra feels his weight congeal against her, hears his breathing slow. She slips out from under him and he slumps sideways onto the couch. Popcorn rises with her. He shakes like he is wet. He looks at her with need in his eyes.

"All right," she says.

Outside, a full moon hidden by clouds, clouds and water tinted by its light like decorations at a dance. Kendra whistles and pats her hip, leading Popcorn up the boardwalk, his tail batting the air.

Hours later, Dean wakes up on the couch. The room is dark but for the remnants of the fire. Kendra has covered him with an afghan. For a moment, he doesn't know who or where he is. His heart is pounding. His entire life, his very substance, has been erased. Then he hears snoring—Popcorn dozing between the coffee table and the couch—and the world comes back. His heartbeat slows. The October night is still.

Kendra sleeps late on Saturdays, drawing slumber over her head like an extra blanket. Dean plays mixed doubles at the club. He will be home before noon, bearing bags of bread and cheese and cold cuts or shrimp to be boiled or takeout from Miss Lulu's. Bloody Mary mix if they're out. They will eat lunch, nap, then watch Alabama play football on TV.

Still drowsy, she carries the paper out to the porch, perusing the sports page for a question she might ask during the game. Dean takes such pleasure in explaining the minutiae. Popcorn keeps her company for a while, then pads over and stands belly deep in the bay, staring straight down into the water, his face serious, lost in concentration. He's only watching minnows. There was a time when Kendra was jealous of her husband's other women—that's how she thought of them—those short-haired, sturdy-thighed tennis ladies, those tan, midlife athletes, but her jealousy, like all unpleasant things, has faded. Kendra is no tennis player. She is a woman who knows how to set a table, how to make a guest feel welcome in her house, a woman who wears her beauty like an evening gown, her long limbs, her extravagant mouth. There is nothing sporty or offhand about her.

Popcorn stiffens in the water, ears cocked. Dean is home. Even before she hears his tires on the cockleshells, the dog is galloping around the house.

Half a minute later, her husband appears, screen door slapping shut behind him.

"I've got crabmeat. Fresh off the boat."

Kendra rakes her fingers through her hair.

"I haven't even showered."

"This is how I like you best."

She can see Popcorn pressing his nose against the screen.

"Is that a wet dog in my house?"

Dean's eyebrows jump up—surprised, guileless— above his sunglasses. He opens the screen door and Popcorn jangles out, prancing at Dean's knees, Dean thumping his sides.

"You old bad dog," he says. "You old wet dog. No wet dogs inside. You know better than that."

"So do you," Kendra says, displeased by the pettiness in her voice.

"How can I make it up to you?"

She leaves the sports page on the wicker table, pushes to her feet, kisses his cheek.

"Let me take a shower," she says.

What had these mornings been like before her son went off to school, before he was born? She can't recall, not clearly. Instead a memory of hustling Thomas into church clothes leaps to mind, but that's tomorrow and she will have no little boy to cajole. While Dean cuts celery for Bloody Marys, Kendra prepares West Indies salad—lump crabmeat, chopped onions, olive oil, white vinegar. Their life revolves from meal to meal. They let their lunch chill for an hour, then eat it on saltines.

"How did you play this morning?" Kendra says.

Her hair is still damp from the shower. She smells of coconut, roses. Dean's tongue darts out after a fleck of cracker on his cheek.

"My first serve was a little shaky but we won," he says. "Straight sets."

Kendra clears the dishes. Dean loads them in the washer. They walk Popcorn without a leash. He trots along the water's edge, under other people's wharves, back up to the boardwalk to check in with Dean, the bay mud brown now and rough as bark.

At home, Dean brushes his teeth and strips to his boxer shorts, his chest paler than his face and forearms. They make love on cool, clean sheets. Lazy, inconsequential. This, too, a part of their routine. Kendra doesn't think she'll be able to sleep—she's not tired; her day has hardly started— but the Bloody Marys have sapped her strength and before long she is falling, falling, the buzz of an outboard motor fussing in through the screen.

The town of Fairhope was conceived as a kind of utopia, a place where a man might own what he created but the value of the land belonged to all. It was discussed in the journals of the day, visited by artists and intellectuals. Some hundred odd years later, Bay Street is all charming storefronts and cafés. There is art for sale but it's priced beyond the reach of artists. If you didn't know better, you might assume that such a place was dreamed up by a woman like Kendra Walker. In her slacks and blouse. Her hair recently styled. You might assume that you know something about her. She sits in her car outside the salon and instructs a talent agent on her cell. She has booked a band for her husband's party. Dean likes Motown, beach music. He likes to dance. The band will set up in the ballroom of the old hotel. Her son is coming home. On her signal, Kendra tells the talent agent, the band should play "Happy Birthday," then follow it with that famous Otis Redding song. She imagines herself spinning on the dance floor, passed from Dean to Thomas, a rowdy horn section, back-up singers, the night trembling with music and stars.

Rain mists on the windshield. Kendra cradles the phone in her lap. A mother emerges from the bookstore, trailed by two little girls. They are all three wearing yellow raincoats and holding black umbrellas over their heads. The mother is carrying a shopping bag, heavy with new books. They proceed in a row, in order of age, tallest to shortest, one behind the other like ducks. Kendra puts the girls somewhere around ten and six, the mother in her middle thirties. School has just let out. Three doors down, they disappear into the bakery where, in another week, Kendra will place an order for her husband's cake. She dials Dean's direct line on her cell.

"Sweetheart," he says.

"I've got everything settled with the band."

Dean is sitting at his desk with his feet propped up. He didn't realize there was anything left to be settled. His office is in a brownstone on Conti Street, windows overlooking Cathedral Square. Rugs selected by his wife, photos of his son. The sign over the front door reads *Walker and Bolling, Attorneys at Law*. It's embellished with scales of justice designed to look like an anchor or an anchor that resembles scales of justice, depending on your perspective. They specialize in maritime cases, insurance claims relating to ships and cargo, civil matters between ship owners. Dean is almost never called upon to go to trial. They have three associates, four secretaries, two paralegals, and a runner who doubles as the IT guy.

"That's good news," he says.

The rain has already blown over on his side of the bay. On her side, the rain keeps sifting down.

"Everything else all right?" Dean says.

"Everything's fine. I just thought you'd like to know."

He drops his feet to the floor, drifts over to the window. The dome of the basilica rises up above the oaks—beautiful, but Dean has always thought it looks mislaid, too Eastern, not of this place. A homeless man dozes on a park bench in the square.

"Tell you what," he says, "why don't I take us out tonight? We haven't been to Felix's in a while. We'll have turtle soup."

"I don't like turtle soup."

"Of course not. You'll have the bisque."

"I do like bisque," she says.

Kendra can remember her first date with Dean as clearly as last night. It's the long stretch in between that's sometimes difficult to fathom. His friend Louis was married to her friend Mona, and Louis and Mona contrived to fix them up. You have so much in common, they said. Kendra was less than a year removed from Sweet Briar, working as a teller at a bank. Dean was one of forty associates at a big law firm. He had too much to drink at dinner. Kendra lost the keys to her apartment. Each apartment had a small, wrought-iron balcony and Dean proposed that he would climb up the outside of the building and let them in through the unlocked balcony doors.

"You're not serious," she said.

"I am indeed."

"You'll break your neck."

"It's not that high."

"But you're half drunk."

"When I'm half drunk," he said, "I'm twice the man."

It was at that moment, Kendra thinks, that she began to love him. He handed her his sport coat and commenced to climb, inching his way up the rain gutter, swinging his legs over the railing of the first balcony, then the next, like he had scaled at least one tall building every day of his life, that night leading inexplicably, inexorably to this night on the wharf, darkness hovering over the water like mist over a meadow. Moths plink against the overhead, mesmerizing Popcorn. For a moment, he has forgotten the tennis ball lodged between his teeth.

"Thomas called," she says.

"Let me guess: he wants someone to write a check."

"He asked if he could bring a date to your party."

"White girl?" Dean says.

"You hush."

He laughs softly at his own bad joke.

"What'd you tell him?"

"I told him I would speak to you."

"I think it's fine," Dean says. "What's this girl's name?"

And so on through the particulars of the phone call. The overhead bulb has a peculiar, insulating effect. Shadows stretch and lean in the oblong of its radiance, minnows flicking to the surface where light brushes the water. Beyond it, the bay is a pure dark slate. The universe ceases to exist.

* * *

Both of them acknowledge that Dean's party has gotten out of hand. They laugh about it over drinks. You add one name to the guest list and suddenly you've opened a door, crossed a border, and there are a dozen more you must include. In addition to organizing the party, Kendra has purchased a pair of antique cuff links, a shirt from Burke & Daniels, a box of monogrammed handkerchiefs. Dean folds them into the back pocket of his suits. Kendra appreciates the fact that her husband is so old-fashioned. He has an email account for work but refuses to log on. His secretary's first job every morning is to survey his inbox, delete the clutter, print the emails that matter. The image of Dean at his desk reading printed emails swells Kendra's heart. He dictates his responses. His secretary clicks them off into the ether.

And this: he insists on Christmas stockings despite the fact that Thomas is too old. He likes to see them hanging heavy on the hearth. In Kendra's, he puts a hundred little things—bracelets and exotic liqueurs and vials of spices she will never use. Books filled with pithy inspiration. A watch in a velvet box. One-of-a-kind earrings. A wallet, a slender belt.

And this: her husband is faithful. Of that Kendra has no doubt. He brings home the occasional rumor about his tennis buddies or men he knows from work, his voice thick with disappointment. Marriages pull apart around her. But not hers, never hers.

The alarm clock rouses Dean at six AM. He shuts it off and rests a moment on his back, adjusting to the light of a new day, his hand on his wife's warm hip. When the coffee is ready, he pours a cup and sips it in the driveway while Popcorn does his business, the sky hazy and gray. He showers, leaving enough hair in the drain to make him nervous, though he's not really going bald. Towel around his waist, Dean wipes steam from the mirror over the sink, his face always a slight surprise in the misted glass, not because he has forgotten how he looks but because his impression of himself never quite matches the image in the mirror. It's like hearing his own recorded voice, the sound familiar and strange at once. Somehow, the shaving cream on his cheeks makes his features recognizable again. Those are the same eyes that have been staring back at him from mirrors his whole life.

In his closet hang a dozen suits in dry-cleaning bags, his shoes lined up neatly on the floor. He dresses but waits to knot his tie. When Thomas was a boy, Dean would wake his son for school at this point in the ritual, his voice soft but firm, then drink a second cup of coffee on the wharf while Thomas performed his own ablutions. He gathered himself, became himself, in those moments, the view of the bay always the same. Thomas is gone, of course, but habit carries Dean out to the water, a pelican perched so still atop a channel marker it looks more decorative than alive.

This morning, however, this plain Tuesday morning is different. Yes, Kendra will stir before too long to receive his good-bye kiss and yes, a day of briefs and meetings awaits him at the office, but on this morning, Dean joins that dwindling portion of his fellow citizens who participate in the democratic process. He will cast his vote in the gymnasium of a middle school, the parking lot surrounded by campaign signs. The scene puts him in mind of a Polaroid as he steps out of his car, the colors a trace too bright. Two old white women with yellowing bouffants man the tables inside. Dean waits in line behind a black man in a wheel-chair with a veteran's pin on the brim of his ball cap. In a few hours, Kendra will cancel out Dean's vote but it doesn't matter. He already suspects that his candidate will come up short. He'll win Alabama going away but the swing state independents are breaking left, the resigned Midwest shedding its character at about the same rate that its industries are losing jobs. Even so, he goes through the motions, drawing the curtain aside, pressing the buttons. The old white women wish him well.

Duty done, he steers one-handed west across the bay, low tide exposing islands of mud and marsh grass, cars jostling for position, downtown Mobile revealing itself dead ahead. In five days, it will be official. Dean Walker will have lived for half a century.

*　　*　　*

Brooke Pitman is not the girl her son will marry. Kendra understands this right away. They arrive on the Friday afternoon before Dean's party, Thomas honking his horn in the driveway, stirring Popcorn to near mania. There is something vaguely foreign in the shape of her eyes. She's pretty but only that. Perhaps Kendra is being unfair. Some women don't come into substance until much later. Brooke, a year older than Thomas, spent the previous semester abroad. With one hand over her heart, she speaks of seeing *Titus Andronicus* at the Globe. But she is majoring in Communications. She has a tattoo of a four leaf clover on her ankle.

The house is immaculate. Rosie has been over everything with cloth and polish and feather duster. There are new sheets, washed and ironed, on the bed in the guest room. Thomas wants to show Brooke around. They stroll hand in hand along the boardwalk with Popcorn at their heels. To Kendra, Thomas looks self-conscious holding hands but he does not let go. Kendra sets out pecans and grapes and olives so they will have something to snack on when they return. The lamps, the paintings. The burnished wood. Her house is rich in beautiful things but none can compare to the view at this hour.

By the time Dean comes home from work, the three of them are drinking beer and playing Trivial Pursuit. Even drinking beer his wife is elegant. It's as if she is emitting light. She is almost frightening. The great room shimmers with her presence. She has a bottle in one hand, a game card in the other, slim bracelets dancing on her slim wrist. Thomas slouches easy at the table, Greek letters on his T-shirt. In an act of harmless sedition, he pledged ΣAE last year instead of ΔKE, his father's fraternity.

"This is Brooke," he says, and the young woman stands, smoothes her skirt, presents her hand.

"Welcome," Dean says. "Let me fix a drink."

"Mrs. Walker is winning," Brooke says, meaning the game.

Her hand is warm and damp. Dean leaves his briefcase on a church pew, kisses his wife, hugs his son, moves around the counter to the kitchen, Popcorn nosing the back of his knee.

"Speaking of which," Kendra says, "what did Portuguese explorers christen *O Rio Mar* in the sixteenth century?"

"Don't answer," Thomas says. "This is for a pie piece."

"She's killing us," Brooke says.

The ice, the whiskey. That first sip.

"The Amazon," Dean says.

Thomas and Brooke groan. Dean lets Popcorn lick an ice cube from his palm. The scene before him fills him up. It's not contentment exactly and it's not pride, though those things are mixed in with what he feels. His son needs a haircut but he's found himself a girl. Maybe she likes it long. Thomas has his mother's hair, straight and blond and glossy. Dean takes his place at the table beside his wife, slips his arm around her back.

"You're on my team," Kendra says.

Later, in bed, Dean holds a biography of Abraham Lincoln open on his lap, reading glasses perched on the end of his nose. All that whiskey has made it difficult to focus. Kendra is amending herself with creams and lotions, the bathroom door ajar.

"Well," he asks her, "what do you think?"

"Keep your voice down."

Thomas and Brooke are watching a movie in the great room.

"They can't hear us."

"Just in case," she says.

"I like her."

"She seems nice."

"She's very pretty."

"I suppose."

Kendra emerges in silk pajamas and sits on the edge of the mattress, her back to Dean, her hair drawn over her right shoulder to be brushed, the rim of her left ear exposed.

"They're not in love," she says.

Later still, Kendra hears her son's door creaking open, his footsteps in the hall, their voices hushed and playful. She scoots closer to Dean, rests her head on his chest. His chest rises and falls. She holds him tight as the world goes spinning off beneath their bed.

This old hotel was built in 1856, forty rooms and a restaurant on the tip of Point Clear, the very place a pendant would dangle from a chain. Eight years later, the Confederates commandeered it for a hospital, their gravestones still visible from the 18th tee. The golf course was added in the twenties, more rooms, swanky cottages, the grand ballroom. It's said that F. Scott Fitzgerald was a guest in the new wing, though no photos of his stay exist. The Army Air Corps used the hotel as a training base during WWII, those polite boys removing their boots before entering to preserve the hardwood floors, history shining like wax on every surface, in every room and hall, on the brass-railed bar, windows reflecting wavery images of passing figures, walking paths buckled by the roots of oak trees even older than the hotel.

At the first hint of evening, lights flick on inside and out, drawing the hotel out of the gloom, making it glimmer and shine, a great ship, an ocean liner from another time about to embark upon a long voyage across a wide and tranquil sea. Kendra has already made several trips back and forth from house to ballroom checking in with the event staff, the caterer, the band. Everything proceeds apace. It will be Thanksgiving in two weeks. In her slip, blow-drying her hair, it occurs to Kendra that her wedding was only slightly more elaborate. But the party was Dean's idea. She asked him what he wanted for his birthday and he said food and friends and music, plenty to drink. She'd been thinking of a trip—Rome or Paris, just the two of them. When she emerges from the bathroom, hair warm against her neck, there is Dean humming as he fingers studs into his tuxedo shirt, and her reservations fall away. This party is not a black-tie affair. The other men will be wearing blazers and slacks, shirts open at the collar. Dean pretends he's sporting his tux ironically but Kendra knows he likes the way it looks.

"I don't want there to be any question," he says, "just who's the man of honor at this shindig."

With Thomas and Brooke, they open Dean's presents and drink champagne in the great room, a private moment before the party. Dean makes a fuss over his gifts. Even Brooke has brought him something, an Alabama jersey with the number 50 on both sides, purchased at the campus bookstore.

"It's nothing," Brooke says. "A token."

Her modesty is becoming. Her calves are taut in her high heels. Her youth makes Kendra's heart race. Thomas beams, already on his third glass.

Then, finally, it's time to go. Night has fallen. Kendra sends Thomas and Brooke on ahead to greet the early arrivals, headlights even now brushing back the darkness. The valets will have their hands full. More people are coming than Kendra could have guessed. Her husband is that esteemed. His partner, Arthur Bolling, will be present, along with all three of their associates. There will be clients like Walter Willett, who runs a tugboat operation, and A.B. Ransom, who owns a shipbuilding concern. His wife, Muriel, is one of Kendra's favorites, a perfect Mobile lady. Erik Nooteboom, whose company transports materials all over the world, is winging in from Denmark. Dean provides counsel for his activities in the Gulf. There will be old friends like Diane and Curtis Henley and Jeb and Posey White and Dean's tennis buddy Paul Saint Clair. Martha and Buddy Bragg accepted the invitation. Their son, Henry, is a fraternity brother of Thomas's at Alabama. Louis and Mona, who finagled Kendra's first date with her husband, will be attending, though they are long divorced. Mona will be unescorted. Louis is bringing his new wife. On and on the guest list goes—Isaac and Hannah Yates, Ellen and Charlie Caldwell, Marcus Weems, whose wife is sick with cancer—names mapping the itinerary of their marriage.

Popcorn shimmies and whines, nuzzling their limp fingers, their clothes. He is aware that something out of the ordinary is afoot. He is right to suspect that he will be left out. "Sorry, boy," Dean says, easing the door closed, the dog mashing his wet nose against the glass.

Arm in arm, Dean and Kendra make their way along the boardwalk. Their house is only six driveways from the old hotel. The night is crisp enough to mist their breath, moonlight glinting on the bay like broken glass.

"You look beautiful," Dean says, and Kendra says, "So do you."

They pass on beneath the oaks, branches draped with moss. Suddenly, Dean is nervous. It's like the dream in which he enters a courtroom unprepared. He has made a mistake. His tuxedo is absurd. He has no idea what he will say to his guests. There is nothing important left to talk about. A dozen bicycles lean in a rack, waiting for hotel guests to claim them. The flag is lifeless on its pole. There is no wind, no chatter of insects.

At last the famous ballroom emerges from the night, all delicate light and lofty windows, guests already mingling beyond the glass, waiters passing hors d'oeuvres. The voices from inside reach them muted and obscure, another frame sliding forward in Dean's dream, the one where everyone is speaking a language he cannot understand.

"Wait," Kendra says, tugging his arm.

"What is it?"

"Just look," she says. "They're here for you."

All those familiar faces. It's like gazing into the past. Elbow to elbow at the bar, Buddy Bragg and Charlie Caldwell and Isaac Yates wait for their drinks, their wives standing to one side. Paul Saint Clair is talking Alabama football with Curtis Henley. There is only one subject in the fall that could make their faces so intent. Behind them, Thomas and Brooke are laughing at something A.B. Ransom has just said. Decorous Muriel swats her husband's bicep. The joke must have been unseemly. Thomas's teeth flash when he laughs, the crooked incisors of his childhood straightened long ago.

And here are Dean and Kendra Walker alone together in the dark. She kisses his jaw, wipes the lipstick print with the heel of her hand. His rush of nerves is passing. He just needs a drink, that's all. On their wedding day, Dean convinced a bridesmaid to slip Kendra a note. *It's not too late. We can still elope.* Kendra held onto it for years. She kept it in a box with tarnished hinges, along with other personal souvenirs—a matchbook, a mateless earring, a ticket stub. Now it is too late. It's far too late. Faintly, from back the way they've come, they can hear Popcorn barking, the sound of him shrill and brokenhearted. They must stay this course until the end.

grand old party

Finding the address is as easy as the Internet. Howell Tate. 1414 Druid Lane. Ivy on the bricks. The neighborhood a dream of landscaping and old houses. Older oaks. The 12-gauge in your hands couldn't feel more out of place. No sign of your wife's car but maybe she parked in the garage. Use the barrel to ring the doorbell. This is what a man does when he's been made a fool.

Inside, a dog barks at the sound, and a moment later, a shadow moves behind the leaded glass and a moment after that, the door swings open to reveal Howell Tate. Must be him. He's wearing khaki pants and a bathrobe open over his bare chest, holding a black standard poodle by the collar.

The poodle bucks and strains, nails ticking on the hardwood. Howell Tate takes in the shotgun and puts his free hand in the air.

"Don't shoot, all right?" He drags the poodle back from the door and bobs his head as if to agree with some point that you have made. "I'll put the other hand up when you're inside. If I let go now Clarence T here is long gone and I'm already in hot water with the neighbors."

When you ask if he knows who you are, he says, "I thought you were the Chinese food but I'm beginning to have my doubts."

When you identify yourself, he says, "Riiight," stretching the word into a lazy drawl. He's stalling, sorting through the situation as he speaks. He's handsome enough, close to your age, fifty-something but fit, plenty of hair, face creased in a way that ruins women but looks OK on a man. During the run-up to election day, your wife and Howell Tate volunteered for the local chapter of the GOP, pestering people over the phone about fundraisers and rallies. All for nothing, it turns out—Obama is still sleeping in the White

House—but Howell Tate kept calling and your wife kept answering, and on the drive over here, when you tried to picture the other man in Hannah's life, you saw him posed before an American flag like an image from a campaign ad.

Tate starts nodding again. "I think I get the picture," he says. "I'd say we're looking at a misunderstanding of some kind." His voice is respectful but unafraid and you can't help admiring his composure.

Tell him you've checked the call history on Hannah's phone. Tell him she carries the phone into the bathroom when it's him. Tell him she's dropped his name a few too many times, as in "Howell Tate thinks Florida's in play this year" or "Howell Tate believes it's a mistake to cozy up to the moderates." Don't tell him how the sight of her makes you feel. Whatever you do don't tell him that. Tell him to turn around. Tell him you want to look upstairs. Tate will do as he is told.

Clarence T bounds ahead, then waits, panting, on the landing. You trail a few steps back. You doubt Tate will try anything but it's probably best to keep your distance just in case.

He glances over his shoulder. "You a hunter?"

Don't answer.

"That's a nice piece," Tate says.

You have been married thirty-one years, decent years, not perfect but good enough. You have three children, two boys and a girl. Douglas, after Hannah's father, and Weyland, after yours, and the youngest, Marianne, all of them married and living their own lives. No grandchildren yet but surely those will come. Hannah has her volunteer work, plenty of friends. You own a string of hardware stores. You've added two locations to the original, established by your father more than sixty years ago, and you're proud of that, no matter that the big chains have chipped your profits down to nothing. You give money to charity. You don't cheat on your taxes. You vote the party line. Barely an hour ago, you were sitting in the dark at the kitchen table, running all this through your head, when that hollowness in your stomach, the feeling that's been nagging you since suspicion first took root, gave way to something more dense, something altogether darker than the kitchen, and you retrieved your side-by-side from the attic. Tate's right. It's a beautiful weapon. Black walnut. Engraved plates.

Tate says, "I want you to know I'm a staunch advocate of the Second Amendment," and right then, a door opens at the end of the hall and there's Hannah in her bra and half-slip, hugging her arms, her hair a mess, her whole body gone soft with age, but still beautiful, still capable of inspiring desire, all of her silhouetted by the lamplight at her back. The fact that she doesn't speak makes her appearance even more startling, as if she's not herself at all but a vision of herself, an image from some uneasy dream.

Clarence T trots around the bedroom from Tate to Hannah to you, sniffing knees and whining like he understands that something important is underway but he's not sure what it is or what's expected of him now. Eventually, he settles at his master's feet and swipes at an itch behind his ear, clinking the ID tag on his collar.

"I don't blame you for being pissed," Tate says. "She's your wife. I get that. I think the shotgun's a little much but I'd be pretty hot, too, if I was in your shoes."

He and Hannah are perched on the end of a king-sized bed, a discreet yard of empty space between them. Like it or not, you're obliged to ask how long they've been carrying on. Both Tate and Hannah start to reply then stop out of deference to the other. Tate waves for Hannah to go ahead. She raises her eyes. Her gaze is frank and sad.

"This is only the third time. I don't suppose that makes a difference."

Don't admit that you're relieved.

"I'm sorry," she says. "I don't guess that makes a difference either."

Then Tate says, "Of course it does. Of course it makes a difference."

Hannah says, "Just quit, Howell. Please."

"All right," Tate says, "but look, we're all grown-up here. These things happen. Doesn't mean anybody should get shot."

Just then, the doorbell rings and Clarence T scrambles to his feet, already barking, and bolts out of the room.

"That'll be the Chinese food," Tate says.

He claps his hands on his knees, makes as if to stand. Remind him that you're armed. Tell him not another word.

Softly, Hannah says, "You're not gonna shoot anybody. You're not that kind of man," and even though what you hear in her voice is more like affection than contempt, tell her you didn't think she was the kind of woman to be unfaithful but here she is and here you are and you never know what a person will do so could she please, please, please, please, please, if she ever really loved you, now would be the time to shut her mouth.

The world is quiet for a second before the doorbell rings again. Clarence T's bark echoes up the staircase in reply. He sounds revived. Warning off strangers, that's something a dog can get his head around.

Tate raises his eyebrows in a question, turns his hands palm-up.

In some more pragmatic chamber of your mind you understand that allowing Tate to answer the door is a bad decision—surely the deliveryman will go away, surely there are mix-ups and prank calls all the time—but mostly you're thinking here's an opportunity to get the night moving forward again, no matter where it leads. You instruct Tate and Hannah to stand, march them single file into the hall and down the stairs. You install Hannah on the sofa in the living room, then take a position where you can keep an eye on your wife and monitor the door.

"All set?" Tate says.

You nod and Tate opens the door and just like that, Clarence T is gone, skittering out between the deliveryman's legs. The deliveryman is, in fact, Chinese. An old guy with too many moles and a scraggly goatee. He watches Clarence T vanish into the dark, then holds up a paper sack and reads from a receipt stapled to the side.

"One orange beef, one General Chin chicken, two spring roll, one snow pea, one wonton soup."

"You got fortune cookies in there?" Tate says.

The deliveryman says, "Always fortune cookie," and you have the idea that you know what's coming, that you've been expecting it. You're not at all surprised when Tate ducks past the deliveryman and leaps the porch steps in a stride. You bring the shotgun up but your wife is right, you can't pull the trigger and Tate is moving fast besides, head down, zigzagging tree to tree. The deliveryman looks at you, his expression bored, disappointed. How long must a man live before the world is drained of fear and wonder? He's in no hurry. He pays no attention to the shotgun. He just waits, tugging gently on his goatee.

Because your hands are full—Chinese food in one, shotgun in the other—you close the door behind you with your foot.

Hannah says, "It's not right you had to pay for that. There's money in my purse if—"

Don't let her finish. You'll never recover if you do. Tell her that you're hungry. You're not, of course, but you're quite absolutely on fire with rage and humiliation and the last thing you want is to be pitied. Order her into the kitchen. Tell her to make a pot of coffee and when she does, try not to think that she's indulging you. Tell yourself that she really is afraid of what you might do. You prop the shotgun in a corner, set the food on a marble-topped island, hoist yourself onto a stool. While you unpack the cartons, Hannah pulls drawers until she locates a fork and you accept it without meeting her eyes. Take no comfort in the fact that she doesn't know where Tate keeps his silverware.

Hannah says, "He'll get the police."

Hannah says, "Believe it or not, I love you."

Hannah says, "Talk to me. Please. We're into something now. I don't know what to do."

You understand that she wants you to forgive her or condemn her, to acknowledge the gravity of the situation, anything, and you feel like a child sitting there, stirring snow peas with the fork, but you can't imagine what to say, nothing real at least, nothing true, nothing that hasn't been said a thousand times.

"All right," she says. "I know you're hurt. You should be. I need to put some clothes on now." She looks tired. She's pinching the bridge of her nose. "There's no excuse for what I've done," she says, letting her hand fall to her side.

What can you do but let her go? As she passes, Hannah touches your shoulder, fingertips warm through the fabric of your shirt, and you really are hungry all of a sudden. You've never felt so empty in your life. Here's chicken, beef, peas right before your eyes. Spring rolls. Go ahead. Eat. Don't think about the end of your marriage or the probability of jail. Let your mind go slack. You're all consumption. Rice. Wonton soup. You're eyeing a fortune cookie when Clarence T clatters into the kitchen, tail wagging, looking pleased to see you, and you hear Tate's voice down the hall saying, "That's his car out front," and you wonder how much time has passed since Hannah left the room.

Another voice, a woman: "You stay put. I mean you stay right here on this spot until we secure the premises."

Tate says, "Ten-four."

Footsteps thudding up the stairs.

Still not thinking exactly, still operating on the surface of yourself, you wipe your mouth and retrieve the shotgun and open the back door. Something stops you at the threshold. Perhaps it's the pool, rimmed with slate, lit up like it's filled with neon, a little waterfall going in the shallow end. In the moment of your indecision, Clarence T shoulders past you into the yard and prances around the perimeter of the privacy fence and you realize that you can't bear to leave your wife alone with this man, Tate. Duck into the walk-in pantry on your left. Press your eye against the door seam. You can make out a half-inch sliver of the kitchen. A few minutes pass before a policeman edges around the corner, does a quick survey of the room, holsters his pistol. He's big, soft-looking, face round and pink, forearms doughy beneath his sleeves. You lose sight of him when he moves off toward the island.

"All clear," he says.

Another cop appears a moment later, a black woman, smaller than her partner by at least ten inches and a hundred-some-odd pounds, younger by ten years.

"You sure?"

"Back door's wide open." His voice is muffled and blurred like he has something in his mouth and you know he's snacking on the remnants of the Chinese food. "Must have fled on foot."

"Hell," the woman says.

"At least there's coffee."

The woman looks at him a moment with her lips pursed, part irritated, part amused.

"Tell me something, Hildebran," she says. "What do you think about all this?"

"All what?"

"These old white people carrying on."

The man doesn't answer right away and you picture him gazing out the door into the night, chewing thoughtfully, mulling the insect sounds, shrill as whistles, and all that ambient light: floodlights, pool lights, porch lights, moonlight, the warm light of other people's windows.

"Everybody's crazy," he says. "Especially in love."

An hour after the police have gone, you're still hiding in the pantry. It's dark in there but for a rectangle traced in light around the door. The shelves are mostly empty. The air smells like dog food and trash bags. Now that some time has passed you can appreciate the absurdity of your situation. It would have been better all around if you'd given yourself up. You've never committed a crime. You're what people call a pillar of the community. You've been trying to come up with a way to extricate yourself without making your presence known—that would only put you right back where you started and this whole night has been a bad idea—but all you can think of is to wait until they go to bed. Your back aches from standing so you lower yourself quietly to the floor and cradle the shotgun in your lap.

Listen.

"I can't believe he ate all this," Tate says. "It's not enough to bring a shotgun in my house, to threaten my life?"

"He wouldn't have hurt anybody," Hannah says.

"He had a gun. I don't think I'm going out on a limb when I assume he meant to use it."

"You don't know him."

"I know he ate my orange beef."

"He paid for it," Hannah says.

"Look," Tate says after a moment, "maybe you'd feel better if you spent the night in a hotel. My treat. I think maybe that's a good idea."

When Hannah doesn't answer, he says, "This isn't what I bargained for."

You understand what's come to pass. How strange to bear witness as this man dismisses your wife, at once tragic and enraging and a source of vindication. All that food, it's like gravel in your stomach. In the silence that follows, you can hear Clarence T scratching to be let in from the yard.

"I can't believe I let this happen," Hannah says, but even as she speaks, you have a sense of sagging down through the layers of how you're supposed to feel, blood rushing in your ears as if from the swiftness of your descent, to some truer, deeper reservoir of feeling in which you are liable for the sadness you can hear in Hannah's voice. Think of all those quiet hours that seemed to you like peace. How is it possible you overlooked her discontent?

"Pass me that fortune cookie," Tate says.

You expect him to read it aloud but he only makes a noise in his throat and Hannah has to ask him what it says.

"It's blank." He sounds surprised. "Somebody fouled up on the assembly line somewhere in the People's Republic. The Party will not be amused."

Clarence T whines and scratches.

"Let the dog in," Hannah says.

A moment later, the door creaks open and you hear Clarence T skitter in over the tile, hear him make a happy lap around the island. When he swipes at the pantry, your bones go brittle in your skin.

"Here's what we'll do," Tate says. "I'll take you to the Radisson and you can stay there on me until your husband is in custody. Then we'll meet for dinner one night, do proper good-byes."

"I have my car. I'll just go home."

"The police didn't think that was the best idea."

"I'm not afraid," she says.

Clarence T paws the pantry door again and you push to your feet. Your knees and ankles pop, as loud to your ears as snapping fingers, but neither Tate nor Hannah comments on the sound.

"Don't make this harder than it has to be, Hannah. I didn't set out to hurt you. Your husband showed up with a gun."

"You're a coward," Hannah says. "You left me here."

"I went for help," Tate says.

Hannah laughs and you can hear that she is close to tears. "Say what you want about my husband, you can't call him a coward. I think it's romantic what he did."

"That's one way of looking at it," Tate says.

Again, the scrape of claws.

"Feed your dog," Hannah says. "I'm going home."

Her sandals slap as she storms out of the room. It's easy enough to imagine Tate on the other side of the door. He's got one hand on his brow as if checking for a fever and his cheeks are puffed with air. He's wondering how he got himself into such a mess as this.

"Clarence T, my old friend," he says, "I'm just not sure it's worth it."

The thing to do is to be waiting with your hands up when Tate opens the door. Your wife is headed home, despite everything, and you're a good man in your heart. But the weight of the shotgun is somehow reassuring, something to hold on to, the trigger slim and cold as jewelry to the touch, and you can't convince yourself to put it down. Crazy, that policeman said. Romantic, Hannah said. You have the idea that this night has been bearing down on you forever and as the knob begins to turn, you can feel your whole life funneled hard into the here and now: nothing before this moment, nothing after.

the king
of dauphin island

Marcus Weems was the sixth richest man in the state of Alabama but he lost his wife to cancer like everybody else. Of course he brought the full leverage of his affluence to bear on her condition—Sloan Kettering, Johns Hopkins, MD Anderson, names of hospitals like the board of directors for some conglomerate of suffering—but the diagnosis had come too late, all the treatments and the clinical trials for naught, and Suzette Weems died at home with her family at her bedside, the day's last light outside her windows reflected on Mobile Bay.

In addition to her devoted husband, Suzette Weems was survived by two daughters: Meredith, twenty-nine, wife of Harris Stokes and mother of infant James; and Emily, twenty-one, treasurer of Kappa Kappa Gamma sorority at the University of Alabama. They were capable and well-adjusted girls, achingly dear to Marcus. After the funeral, Emily requested incompletes in her fall classes and resumed permanent occupancy of her room, perfuming the house with the lavender and praline bouquet of her shampoo. At least three nights a week, with infant James in tow, Meredith abandoned her husband to sleep over as well, regularly enough that she stocked the empty bureau of her youth with diapers and onesies and nursing bras. Marcus thought he understood. They believed that their presence would provide a bulwark against his loss. They loved him and he loved them back and he was willing to humor them for a while. Together, they strolled the Point Clear boardwalk, gulls wheeling, infant James strapped to one of them by a contraption that put Marcus in mind of a papoose. They played backgammon in the evenings and Marcus let them win, as he had when they were children. The holidays passed in a haze of dirty dishes and wads of wrapping paper and strained good cheer. Marcus was sixty-eight years old. He'd started late on marriage, fatherhood. He'd wanted to be certain that he was prepared to do it right. And he had. Just look at his magnificent daughters. But now, at night, when everyone was asleep, he found himself creeping from room to room in the dark, picking up letter openers and coffee table books and putting them down again like he'd forgotten what they were for.

In January, he nudged Emily back to school and convinced Meredith that her husband required her attention. They went reluctantly but they went, casting worried glances through the rear windshields of their cars. Marcus had, in the course of his career, parlayed a modest inheritance into a fortune in commercial real estate. His holdings included a condominium complex on Dauphin Island, a barrier island off the coast. Without informing his daughters, he put his house on the market—a pocket listing, priced to move—let the condo manager know he was coming, and drove alone across the bridge over the Sound. The

Admiral's Quarters rose up from the sand where the beach was at its widest. Marcus claimed a corner unit on the fourth and highest floor. Two bedrooms. One bath. Combined kitchen and living area. Every accoutrement tastefully bland. Among real estate professionals, it is a widely held belief that beach rentals, especially condominiums, are rarely haunted by anything more than the detritus of previous guests—those battered paperbacks, that bottle of hot sauce, those loose pennies in a drawer. From his balcony, Marcus could see an old public pier jutting like a ruin over the dunes, the shore tugged out by tides in such a way that the pier no longer reached the waves.

His daughters were predictably stunned by this turn of events, not to mention wounded, furious, concerned, and a number of additional sentiments, which they expressed in weepy monologues over the phone. Marcus could hear the wind whining around the building as they spoke and the distant hissing of the surf, sounds indistinguishable from his tinnitus, a cocoon of white noise that made it difficult to focus on his daughters. Didn't he realize, Emily wanted to know, that they had lost their mother, too? Shouldn't he have at least consulted them, Meredith demanded, before listing the house? They had a talent for phrasing questions in such a way that the answers were implied. And they were right. His behavior was selfish and impulsive and thoroughly out of character. Daddy, they called him. Still. Like little girls.

He bought a bike, secondhand, from a rental shop down the road, a lady's bike, though Marcus didn't mind, a lipstick-red Schwinn Hollywood Roadster, handlebars outfitted with a bell and basket, everything but the basket freckled with rust. Dauphin Island is bisected, lengthwise, by Bienville Boulevard, twelve miles of sandy pavement paralleled by sidewalk. Down this sidewalk rode Marcus Weems. Exploring. Acclimating. As if the island were a scale model of his life without Suzette, or of the space left inside him by her absence and he wanted to plot its boundaries. Mornings, he rode to Lighthouse Bakery for a cup of coffee and a bear claw. He rode to Pirate's Booty Bait and Dry Goods in the afternoon to stock up on peanut butter and white bread. The west end of the island had been stripped of all but the most obdurate shrubbery by careless development and countless storms, nothing down there anymore but vacation homes on stilts and a ribbon of beach visible only at low tide. One day, Marcus counted twenty-six for-sale signs. The day after that, he counted twenty-nine. Most of the year-round residents were hunkered down on the east end, tucked in along the Sound or on the leeward side of the dunes. Marcus coasted past their houses, pulled lazy U-turns in their cul-de-sacs. He rode past Dauphin Elementary, the only school on the island, and past Cadillac Park, live oaks dripping beards of Spanish moss, and past the bird sanctuary where so many weary species, headed north for warmer months, first caught sight of land. He kept on riding until he ran out of boulevard, all the way to Fort Gaines, best remembered by history for its failure to prevent the Yankee fleet from breaching Mobile Bay.

Here, Marcus dropped the kickstand and dismounted. Like the long-gone captains of the Confederacy, he stood watch at the edge of Dauphin Island, his old life just out of sight across the water. What he felt in those moments, pelicans skimming the chop, tankers lugging cargo to ports unknown, was not loneliness or loss, as you might expect, not the weight of tragedy but its opposite, pure lightness, the hole left inside him by Suzette's death as big and hollow as a zeppelin and just as buoyant, as if the shape of her absence might lift him up and carry him away.

Near the end of his first week on the island, after a particularly exhausting call from Meredith, Marcus crossed Bienville Boulevard on foot to Dauphin Bar and Grill, one of three yellow A-frames huddled in a gravel parking lot. The other two housed Island Ice and Slice, a snow cone and pizza joint, and Massacre Island Surf Shop, so named because in 1699 the explorer Pierre Le Moyne dropped anchor long enough to misinterpret the nature of a mound of human bones—most likely the burial site of some forgotten tribe—and leave the island with that short-lived but gruesome designation. These three establishments, Marcus would soon discover, were owned and operated by three brothers: Alton, Ike, and Homer Tenpenny. Homer doubled as the mayor of Dauphin Island.

He found the Tenpennys posted up at the bar, along with half a dozen local drunks, the walls adorned with Crimson Tide football paraphernalia and faded photographs of men with fish. Marcus helped himself to a table by the window and eavesdropped while they griped. For fifteen minutes, no one acknowledged his arrival. Finally, Homer interrupted the discussion long enough to take Marcus's order—burger, well-done—and pass it through to the kitchen before returning to his place behind the taps and picking up the conversation where he'd left off. Favorite subjects included liberals, immigrants, and tourism revenue in steep decline, each topic a different route to the same conclusion: every single thing was going to hell. If the Tenpennys could be believed, the population of Dauphin Island was down at least two hundred souls the last few years, the island itself shrinking all the time, erosion caused by dredging in the ship channel.

"By the time I'm gone," Homer said, "won't be nothing left."

Marcus appreciated the resignation in their anger. He took a curious sort of pleasure in the redundancy of their complaints. These men—or men like them—had been having this conversation —or one like it—forever and would go on having it until their dire prognostications came true at last. Marcus added a memorable tip to his bill and retired to his condo for a nightcap on the balcony, natural gas wells burning way out in the Gulf like the first glimmers of an inkling, like the signal fires of his grief.

In the morning, he showered and shaved and biked along Bienville Boulevard to the local real estate office. The adjacent storefronts—a former video game parlor and a former gift shop and a former kayak rental place—were all defunct. Marcus ducked inside behind the tinkling of a bell. The realtor, Norma Bird, according to the nameplate on her desk, flinched at the sound, one hand going to her chest, her glasses slipping down her nose. She had been feeding papers into a shredder.

"I'd like to inquire about some property," he said.

By Marcus's standards, real estate on Dauphin Island was remarkably inexpensive. He'd have to move some funds around, divest himself of some investments, but by the time he'd left the office, proceedings had been initiated on the purchase of the twenty-nine available houses on the west end, along with an out-of-business barbecue restaurant called the Salty Pig, a twelve-unit motel on the Sound, fourteen additional houses on the east end, and all three available storefronts in the strip mall. As Marcus was signing the last of the paperwork, Norma Bird reached out and gently poked her index finger into his ear and he started like she'd given him a pinch.

"I'm sorry." She barked out a laugh and covered her mouth as if shocked by what she'd done.

"That was totally inappropriate. Totally, totally, totally. This is just so unreal."

Marcus supposed it wasn't very often that the sixth-richest man in the state strolled into her office and offered to buy every listing on the island. A measure of shock could be expected and forgiven. He spent the remainder of the afternoon on the phone with lawyers and moneymen, the hair in his ear retaining a faint, residual tickle from her touch. He was in his kitchen, later, pouring bourbon over ice and boiling hot dogs and listening to Mozart's Concerto no. 4 in E-flat Major on CD when the doorbell chimed. He drifted in that direction, sipping the drink, his second of the evening, his mind swimming with whiskey and music and the vaguest beginnings of a plan. There were state and federal permits to sort out and he'd have to sell off a shopping mall to foot the bill, but Marcus had plenty of industry and government connections and as he pressed his eye to the peephole, it all seemed possible, whatever it was. There in the hall, distorted by the lens, stood the Tenpenny brothers. Ike smoothed a palm over his hair. Alton straightened the lapels of a madras blazer. Homer pressed his eye against the peephole on his side, blotting out the view.

"You're the big tipper," he said, when Marcus opened the door.

Marcus invited them in, set everybody up with a drink. He offered to throw a few more hot dogs in the pot but they declined. They sat at a table on the balcony in unseasonable warmth and Marcus waited for the Tenpennys to get down to business. There were no sunset beachcombers leaving footprints in the sand.

"Norma Bird came by," Homer said. "I guess we're here because we'd like to know your intentions."

His brothers nodded. Alton's neck was spotted with razor burn and Marcus wondered if he'd spruced himself up for this meeting.

"I want to buy the island."

"Uh-huh. I see. And what do you mean to do with it?"

"I'm not sure about that," Marcus said.

Homer pursed his lips and stared for a moment into his drink.

"This is a community," he said, raising his eyes.

"It's dying," Marcus said. "It's nearly dead."

The Tenpenny brothers were quiet. They had no rebuttal. Marcus went back inside the condo, leaving them with their thoughts. He found a pen and jotted a figure on the back of a takeout menu from a seafood restaurant that had gone belly up years ago. He refilled his drink, returned to the balcony, and slid the menu across the table. Ike retrieved a pair of bifocals from his breast pocket so he could read it.

"That's how much I'll give you for the A-frames," Marcus said.

Ike held the menu close to his glasses, then backed it away as if trying to bring an optical illusion into focus.

Marcus told them he would understand if they needed time to consider his offer. He explained that he had experience with loss. In the end, they polished off their drinks and shook his hand to seal the deal.

*   *   *

Massacre Island was eventually renamed for the great-grandson of Louis XIV, the twenty-third Dauphin, a frivolous and empty-headed prince who would become a dreadful king. Because of its deep-water harbor, the island served as a port for the territory of French Louisiana but even then, even three hundred years ago, shifting sands were conspiring to fill in the harbor. The settlement was burned to the ground by Jamaican privateers in 1717, leveled twice more that century by hurricanes. After the Civil War, the history of the island, like its present, is unmemorable, marked primarily by personal tragedies and low-budget vacations and a gradual but inevitable wearing away.

Marcus wheeled the Schwinn up and down Bienville Boulevard seeing not scruffy houses clinging like barnacles to the fringe of a vanishing beach but the empty, windswept shores of his imagination. Demolition costs would be exorbitant but not, he didn't think, out of reach. He'd have to unload an office park or two, maybe borrow against some undeveloped land. One of his lawyers had turned up a Corps of Engineers proposal to truck one-hundred-million tons of sand onto the island as backfill against the past and buffer against the future. The state would never fund such an extravagant conservation scheme, but Marcus could. He pictured houses tearing themselves down and hauling their parts away, the wind and tides giving back the beach, Dauphin Island rising unblemished from the Gulf like time-lapse film run in reverse.

In this new light, the light of evening and recollection and caprice, the island looked newly beautiful to Marcus, that useless old pier a monument as profound as the Parthenon, the tufts of seagrass sprouting from the dunes a reminder not of the futility of life but its tenacity.

He saw no benefit to telling his daughters about his plan. He knew what they would have said. They were good girls. They would have tried to reason with him. They might have loved him half to death. So he deleted their emails and let their messages pile up in his voice mail. Sometimes, at night, alone in his condo, he could almost hear their trapped voices straining to reach him through the line, and though a part of him longed to hear his daughters speak, he was afraid that if he let himself listen to even one message, the rest would come flooding out behind it and he would drown in their good sense. His youngest daughter became so frustrated that she wrote him a letter, the first he had received from her since summer camp. He couldn't resist slipping a thumbnail under the flap. The letter was penned in a familiar looping script on official Kappa Kappa Gamma stationery, Emily's name third from the top in the chapter masthead. In its pages, she added *confused* and *abandoned* to the list of feelings she had expressed over the phone. She worried that Marcus had become *unhinged by grief,* a poetic phrase out of character for such a practical young woman, the treasurer of a sorority. He pictured her laboring over the line at her little desk in her little room at the Kappa Kappa Gamma house, early drafts wadded in the trash can by the door. She didn't know the half of it, Marcus thought.

Norma Bird had started the paperwork on fifty-two more houses, the marina, the service station, the bakery, the seafood market, a nine-hole golf course, and all eleven churches on the island, each new purchase pouring a little more substance back into Marcus, filling him up again. Technically, the public beaches and the parks and the bird sanctuary were not for sale, but an exploratory conference call with the governor left the impression that the state of Alabama, which had enough financial woes without sweating the overhead on Dauphin Island, was open to creative fiduciary arrangements. There were a handful of holdouts among the locals but Marcus was sure they'd come around. You will be hard-pressed to find a real estate operator savvier than Marcus Weems. He had learned over time that three things were necessary in any delicate transaction. First, you had to offer a fair price, one that benefited buyer and seller equally. Next, you had to convince the seller that his position was untenable, as in his many negotiations with struggling farmers and sons of struggling farmers reluctant to forsake the family land. Last—and this was

Marcus's true specialty, the reason he succeeded where others failed—it was incumbent upon the buyer to make the seller believe that the transaction would leave a legacy he could be proud of.

Marcus bought round after round of drinks at Dauphin Bar and Grill, the place crowded every night now and not only because someone else was picking up the tab. He spun for his audience a vision of the island returned to its right and natural state. On cocktail napkins, Norma Bird kept track of the tipsy offers Marcus was prone to make on these occasions. When he'd had a few too many, he tended to go on about his wife, how beautiful she had been, how wise, how all his money failed to save her.

"I proposed four times before she said yes. Once I chased her all the way to San Francisco. Her sister lives out there. I showed up at the door with a string quartet and a diamond big as your fist but still she turned me down. That was the third time. She said I only wanted what I couldn't have. You believe that? Me standing in the middle of Lombard Street, two thousand miles from home."

Homer Tenpenny patted him on the back. "Time to settle up," he said.

The next day, it began to rain and did not stop for a full week, a misty, spitting rain interspersed with downpour that rendered the Gulf invisible from Marcus's balcony. His view reached no farther than the end of the old pier. He swam his slow Australian crawl in the indoor pool and wondered what to do with the Admiral's Quarters. The complex would be a blemish once the island was restored but if he tore it down, where would he live? In the sauna, sweat running in his chest hair, he entertained fantasies of living in a teepee or digging some sort of bunker, but he recognized these idylls for what they were and blamed them on the heat. At dinnertime, he popped his umbrella and hustled over to Dauphin Bar and Grill. The rain had chased the crowds away but Norma Bird was nursing a beer two stools down from one of the holdouts, a ship's captain who owned a saltbox with crooked shutters on the Sound. Peebles something? Something Peebles? Marcus recognized the locals by their property but had trouble recalling their names. This man was close to Marcus's age but had no wife, no children, no reason to stay except inertia and lack of imagination.

"I've been here a long time," he said.

"But it won't be *here*," Marcus replied, "once everybody else is gone."

Peebles something shrugged and thanked Marcus for the beer and Marcus proceeded to drink himself into such a stupor that Norma Bird insisted on walking him home. Their hips bumped under his umbrella, her arm around his waist, rain beating on the pavement all around them. Halfway across the street, she stopped and turned to face him. She palmed his cheek. "You'd never know it to look at you," she said, and though he didn't understand exactly what she meant, he understood that a great deal more was implied. Her very nearness startled him, sobered him. His breath misted her glasses. For a long few seconds, Marcus covered her hand with his own. Then he left her standing under his umbrella in the rain.

* * *

He was on his way back from Norma Bird's office one afternoon when he noticed Emily's Land Rover, the car he'd bought as a high school graduation present, idling in front of the Admiral's Quarters.

Emily spotted him on his bike.

"Daddy, is that you? I see you. Daddy, you get over here right now."

He rolled up beside her car, ringing the bell on his handlebars in greeting.

"You're in big trouble," Emily said.

Despite the angry words, she let him kiss her cheek. Meredith was in the backseat with infant James.

"You'd better let us in," she said. "I need somewhere to nurse the baby."

Marcus thumbed the code on the keypad and pedaled through the security gate into the parking garage, Emily's Land Rover at his heels. Once inside the condo, Meredith fished a newspaper clipping from her purse. The headline: *Mysterious Land*

Grab by Local Real Estate Tycoon. The article included a photograph of Marcus. He remembered when it was taken. Maybe ten, twelve years ago. Before Suzette's diagnosis. Their house had been featured in a lifestyle magazine. In the photograph, he looked awkward but game. The newspaper had cropped Suzette out of the shot.

"What on earth?" Emily said.

"I'm sorry you had to hear this way. I really am."

"You're a mess, Daddy," Meredith said. "That's why we came."

Infant James was at her breast. Marcus had never felt comfortable in the presence of a woman nursing a baby, especially not his daughter. He directed his gaze out the sliding glass doors to the balcony, an evasion that made him look guilty, though that was not the way he felt.

For an hour, Marcus listened while his daughters pleaded their case, first Meredith, then Emily, sometimes both at once, their voices twining in his ears, his eyes focused on the breakers rolling ceaselessly up onto the beach. Theirs was not, he understood, an unreasonable position. They addressed him as respectfully as he could have hoped, given the circumstances. He refused to believe that he could lose them over this. Finally, Meredith tucked her breast back into her blouse and Emily concluded their remarks. "This is not what Mother would have wanted."

Marcus hesitated. Such sensible girls.

"I was thinking I would have your mother reinterred. There's a beautiful little cemetery on the Sound."

Emily burst into tears. She covered her face with both hands and made a noise like a squeaky wheel. Meredith stared at her father, perplexed, infant James already sleeping in the crook of her arm.

"There's plenty of money," Marcus said. "You don't have to worry."

Emily dropped her hands into her lap. At the same time, she raised her heels and stomped them down, a gesture that called to mind the outbursts of her adolescence. "Oh, Daddy, how could you be so dumb?"

"Once everything is settled on the island, you'll be welcome to visit. We'll have it all to ourselves."

Meredith put a hand on Emily's shoulder. "We should go. We're sorry to bother you, Daddy." She stood slowly, her eyes never leaving his, as if in the presence of a skittish horse. Pregnancy had filled his oldest daughter out—her hips, her calves. She looked complete to Marcus, grown at last.

"Could I hold the baby?" he said. "Just for a second before you leave."

Meredith balked at offering her child up to her father but she relented. Marcus bounced his sleeping grandson in his arms, breathed him in, the smell of him sweet and plain. Sunlight sifted across his face. Infant James twitched and scrunched his cheeks. His cheeks were smooth and pale, round as Christmas baubles. Marcus wondered, not for the first time, what infants dreamed.

Then came the lawyers and the injunctions and all pending transactions put on hold until matters could be settled by the court. His daughters wanted Marcus declared *non compos mentis*. The documents arrived by UPS. Marcus read the pages carefully, tapped the edges together, and filed them in a kitchen drawer with Emily's letter and his car keys.

He biked down to Fort Gaines, locals waving as he passed, honking their horns. He parked his Schwinn in the shadow of the fort and gazed out across Mobile Bay in the direction of his old house. Even now, perhaps, a buyer was wandering the quiet rooms, footsteps echoing on the hardwood. That house had been designed by the architect Fritz Belmont, Jr., a beautiful setting for what had been a beautiful life by any standard, a place so big and rambling that sometimes Marcus could hear his daughters calling and not know where to find them. Picture him sitting there with Suzette, exchanging a smile, a touch, light streaming in through the windows, Marcus rising from the couch or the kitchen table and following the sound of their voices along the hall or up the stairs, pushing open doors, peeking around corners, knowing, as he moved toward them, that anything they desired, be it comfort or praise or some silly, pretty thing, anything in the world was his to give.

Back at the condo, still smarting with reminis-
cence, he spotted a trio of fishermen set up on
the beach in front of the old pier, rod handles
jammed into the sand. Used to be you could fish
from the rail. Marcus had seen the photographs
on the wall at Dauphin Bar and Grill. In one of
these, the young Tenpenny brothers are posed with
a five-foot bull shark, a crowd of gawkers behind
them, the bull shark sprawled damply across the
planks. Marcus had heard them tell the story,
how they'd taken turns on the reel. Even at high
tide, they would have had to haul the shark ten
feet through nothing but air to wrangle it onto
the pier. A miracle the line didn't break. Marcus
imagined the shark hovering up and up and up,
Tenpennys and gawkers cheering it on. Now these
fishermen whipped their lines out past the surf,
the pier looming at their backs. They waited and
Marcus, on his balcony, waited with them. He felt
like he was watching for a sign. He willed a fish to
strike but nothing was biting. Marcus went back
inside to fix a drink. To their credit, he thought,
his daughters had managed to hold off for this

long, to give him this much rope. In the morning, he got his legal team on the phone.

The hearing took place in Mobile, the county seat. Marcus's lawyers wore the finer suits—sleek grays, deepwater blues. They battered the opposition's expert witnesses, Meredith and Emily watching from the plaintiff's table with tissues crumpled in their fists. Marcus did not love them any less. If anything, he loved them more, loved their certainty and their grave faces, each manifesting a different aspect of their mother—Emily her upturned nose, Meredith her ears, perfectly shaped, like the ears from a drawing in a textbook. Both of them had Suzette's pragmatic eyes. And he felt, quite suddenly, during a particularly contentious back and forth regarding the house on Mobile Bay, the rush and tug of some tremendous force dragging at him like an undertow. He could not be sure if this sensation was born of the hearing itself or the presence of his wife in the features of his daughters or the realization that the bounty of this life is not greater than its disappointments, but he clutched the arms of his chair as if to keep from going down. The courtroom was windowless, drop-ceil-inged, lit by rows of fluorescent bulbs. Beneath the table, anxious litigants had worn the carpet to its backing. The stenographer was missing a button on her blouse. But look—despite everything, his daughters shimmered. They understood nothing. They were trying to save him from himself. They might never forgive him if they failed.

During the lunch recess, Marcus instructed his lawyers to surrender. But he was winning, they as-sured him. Precedent was clearly on his side. Buy-ing Dauphin Island was definitely eccentric and arguably irresponsible but in no way unlawful or provably deranged. Marcus waved away their pro-tests. "Whatever they want," he said. A few hours later, with visible regret, the judge read the settle-ment into the record. Control of Marcus's assets was granted to his daughters, his acquisitions on Dauphin Island rendered null and void.

In the ensuing weeks, Meredith and Emily secured a spot for Marcus at a retirement community for active seniors. He would have his own private cottage, a view of Mobile Bay, access to the therapy he needed. There were grief counselors on staff. Support groups. Amazing how many residents had, in so many different ways, lost someone they loved.

Marcus went along with their plans with quiet dignity. He was younger than his new neighbors but not by much. He played bingo, attended movie night. He took lessons in conversational Spanish and watercolor painting and ballroom dancing. He was popular among the widows, all the more so for his lack of interest. He was not a prisoner. He had his car but Marcus stayed close to the grounds, riding his bike on miles of paths, looping through his memory beneath the pines.

The azaleas bloomed in April. Meredith visited every Tuesday and every Thursday and Marcus was careful to look presentable for her. He had been so busy for so long buying up other people's property, other people's lives, that he took an unexpected comfort in remaking himself to suit his daughters.

Infant James was crawling now.

"He looks like you," Meredith said. "He has your chin."

"He looks like his grandmother," Marcus said.

In May, Meredith and her husband picked Marcus up and they made the pilgrimage to Tuscaloosa for Emily's graduation. Because she'd asked for so many incompletes, the actual diploma would be blank but the university had agreed to let her process with the rest of her class. Marcus took pictures like a proper father and posed for more pictures with his children. He held his grandson in his lap. The sky was clear. The clouds were white. The air reeked of old bricks and cut grass and nostalgia.

Everything as it should be.

Occasionally that summer a family from Birmingham or Atlanta would rent a house on the west end of Dauphin Island or a condo at the Admiral's Quarters. For a day or two, they would be charmed by the rustic quality of the place, the sense that nothing ever changed, but the children would grow bored and that rustic quality would begin to look more down-at-heel. They almost always left feeling sad but relieved, as if headed home from a wake. Fort Gaines was placed on a list of America's Most Endangered Historic Places. Apparently, its walls were sturdy enough to withstand the blasts from Yankee cannons but not budgetary shortfalls and salt air. Alton Tenpenny suffered a fatal heart attack in August. Ike filed for bankruptcy and moved in with his son, a high school baseball coach in Selma. Homer carried on alone. Of all the residents of Dauphin Island, Norma Bird was the most sorry to bid farewell to Marcus Weems, the most disappointed that his vision was never realized. Yes, those commissions would have made her rich but she'd also been inspired by his belief that the island could be restored. Those hot blue days, she played solitaire on her computer, the office so quiet she kept imagining the jaunty ring of a bicycle bell outside. Then, in September, that in-between month, no longer summer, not yet fall, Hurricane Raphael blew in, smashing houses and ripping trees up by the roots and dragging countless tons of sand back out to sea.

landfall

Muriel decided to fill the bathtubs just in case. She got the water running in the master bath first, then crossed the landing to the tub her sons, Angus and Percy, had shared when they were boys. Her daughter, Doodle, had had her own bathroom. The privilege of privacy for Muriel's only girl. Her oldest, Doodle, and her youngest, Angus, were married, had children of their own, lived right next door, in fact, on plots of land she'd deeded them as wedding presents. Her middle child, Percy, was without romantic prospects as far as she knew, without prospects of any kind that she could tell, was still doing whatever he'd been doing these past few months at Horseshoe Bend. She'd had a lot drawn up for him as well and would be pleased to hand it over the minute he decided that this was the life he wanted for himself.

When all the taps were running and all the drains were plugged, Muriel circled back to where she'd started and began to shut off the taps again. She didn't really think she'd need so much water but this hurricane was coming and it was important to keep busy. Idleness in an empty house made way for sadness. After the bathtubs, she would invent another task to occupy her time and then her daughter and her granddaughters would arrive and eventually, the storm would make its entrance and another day would be done. It was always with her now, that sadness, like one of those rare orchids you saw clinging to jungle branches on TV, always blooming in her at unexpected moments, and even on the move, scuffing down the hall toward Doodle's room, the thought of evading it called it into being. *Sadness.* The word itself didn't do the feeling justice. What she felt was a more complicated alchemy of emotion, equal parts grief and loneliness and longing, with measures of resentment and self-pity drizzled in. She had to lean against the wall a minute. Breathe. Her best defense against the feeling was to let herself fret over her children, to become more mother than wife. Than widow. So she worried about the fact that somehow Doodle had never learned to look after herself and that Angus would never live up to his father and that Percy would never, no matter how long she waited, no matter how many prayers she offered up, choose the life she wanted for him, the only life that would make him happy, whether he realized it or not. Exactly the sort of concerns she generally struggled to keep at bay but the only ones substantial enough to beat back the loss of her husband. And after a while the feeling passed, a dark flower closing its petals and tucking itself away.

When the grandfather clock chimed at the bottom of the stairs, Muriel remembered that the taps were still running in her daughter's room. How long had she been standing there? She balled her fists and bit her tongue. She pictured water brimming over the tub, pooling on the tile. She hated acting like a sad old woman. But she was being dramatic. The storm was still a long way off and it would be simple enough to clean the mess and the cleaning would provide one more task to fill her time. That's what she was thinking as she rounded into Doodle's bathroom and the sole of her sandal skidded like a skipped rock across the skin of water on the floor. Her body hung suspended for a moment, neither rising nor falling, as if whatever would happen next remained in doubt, before gravity took note of her and dragged her down.

The office still smelled like his father despite the fact that the old furniture had been carted out and replaced months ago, the carpet pulled, the blinds removed, windows left bare to let more light into the room. Angus worried sometimes that his imagination was playing tricks but he could have sworn he detected his father's presence even now. Cigarettes and aftershave. The smell itself didn't really bother him. There was a peppery mustiness to it that reminded him of the woods. What bothered

Angus was feeling like his father was always look-ing over his shoulder.

He dialed his wife's cell and stood at the bank of windows behind the desk gazing out over the shipyard while he listened to the ringing. Here morning light glinted on the cyclone fence. Here on the tin roof of a warehouse. There it made darting shadows of passing birds. Across the dusty yard, berthed on the moss-green river, loomed the *Kagero*, built for a commercial fishing outfit in Yo-kohama, big enough and solid enough that she looked undisturbed by the imminence of weather. Men hustled around on deck, the only sign of life except for Angus. They had other boats on hand, half-complete or in dry dock for repairs, but there was nothing to be done about them now. The *Kagero* wasn't finished, not quite, but she was sea-worthy, which gave him options, and there was a better than average chance that she'd suffer more damage in port than on the open water. Hurricane Raphael had seemed so hesitant as it blew into the Gulf, drifting toward Mexico for half a day before veering up toward Louisiana like it couldn't make up its mind. All the weather service tracking models had turned out wrong. At present, it looked like the eye of the storm would pass directly over Mobile Bay but most of the forecasters had settled on what amounted to a shrug.

Voice mail. Nora always left her ringer off since the baby. Better this way, he thought. It wouldn't be right to tell Nora over the phone.

When Angus was thirteen years old, his father had put him to work at the shipyard after school. Family tradition. Learn the company from the bottom up. He'd started in the warehouse, doing inventory, cleaning, and maintaining equipment. Nothing dangerous, as insisted on by his mother. Mostly what he remembered was miles and miles of burning line, green and orange hoses that carried oxygen and acetylene to the welding torches. It was his job to sink each hose in a tub of water and run air through it. If it made bubbles, there was a leak, which he'd repair with rubber tape. Though the task was monotonous, Angus recognized the mortal responsibility of his assignment. If he allowed a damaged hose back into the yard,

if a spark from one of the torches came into contact with a leak, the world could become suddenly,
irrevocably aflame. He'd moved out of the warehouse when he was old enough to drive himself
to work. Welding, shipfitting. Percy had already
done his time at the yard and headed off to college
and was on his way toward leaving this life behind.
But Angus had known somehow, even young, even
as a thirteen-year-old with his arms sunk elbow-
deep in a tub of water, that this was the path his
life would take, and that knowledge felt less like
pressure than fate. There was a kind of comfort in
its inescapabilty. He would never have to choose.
His responsibilities had become more complex, of
course, especially since his father's death, but no
more grave to Angus than burning lines and rubber tape.

The *Kagero* was fueled. Fixed for crew. He had
been trying to imagine the boat as part of a con-
struct in one of the word problems he'd loved in
math class as a kid. Two trains approaching at such
and such a speed from such and such a distance.
Word problems transformed the abstraction of

arithmetic into something more concrete, something a boy who was good with numbers anyway could really get his head around. In this case, he had a hurricane, roughly 300 miles wide and 230 miles from shore, twisting forward at 13 knots. Approaching from the opposite direction, at 25 knots full-bore, would be his boat, his at least until he handed her over to the Japanese. If his math was right, they still had time to get the *Kagero* to the western edge of the storm, get the wind behind them, use the hurricane's own force to flee instead of battling it head-on.

He needed to get home. Tell Nora. He didn't have much time to spare. He dropped the phone into his pocket and hurried out into the hall, security lights burning in the stairwell as he descended, his footsteps echoing him past the receptionist's station in the lobby, her desk all squared away as if no hurricane was coming and she would be reporting for work as usual any minute. The full brightness of the sun washed over him when he stepped outside and he waited a moment for his vision to adjust, distant shouts wafting his way from the *Kagero*. As he turned to leave, a breeze kicked up, raising miniature whirlwinds in the dust, and Angus thought he heard a voice calling his name. The breeze passed, the dust settled. Angus listened but the voice did not call out a second time.

The first thing Muriel noticed when she came to was a faint, throbbing pain behind her ear. She must have hit her head on the sink when she went down, blacked out. The second thing she noticed was that she was wet, soaking really, from hair to heels. She could hear the water still running in the tub. Mostly what she felt, beyond the pain and its accompanying dizziness, was acute humiliation. She moved her arms a little, felt the water swirl. Maybe half an inch deep. Cold. It occurred to her that if she could move her arms she could likely stand. So she pushed up on her elbows, rested like that, breathing, letting the light-headedness wash over her until she was steady enough to reach for the lip of the sink and slide her hips back and pull herself into a sitting position, water rushing down her spine from her wet hair, her blouse, water sloshing against the walls. She rested again, let the dizziness rise and fall. One of her sandals was floating behind the commode. The other was still in place on her left foot. She toed that one off as well and gradually, both hands gripping the sink, pulled up to her feet—her hips, her back, her knees and elbows, all of her shaky and in pain. But she was standing now. That was something. There was a phone on her daughter's nightstand. Maybe ten paces away. All she had to do was get there and she'd figure out who to call. She didn't want to bother with an ambulance. How would it look to let herself be seen by strangers in such a state? She braced herself first on the doorframe, then the bureau, lunged the last few steps, letting her momentum carry her to the bed, but when she'd swung her legs up and propped her back against the headboard, she found not a single phone number anywhere in her memory, not the shipyard, not her daughter or her sons, not her friends, not even her own home.

For what felt like a long time, she lay there on Doodle's bed awash in muted panic. The panic was not a response to pain, which was bearable, as long as she kept still, but to this troubling emptiness of mind. Muriel had always prided herself on being a resourceful woman. She understood that she needed to do something about her situation but hadn't the slightest idea what that something should be. She closed her eyes and linked her fingers in her lap and concentrated on a memory more rote even than phone numbers, something she could remember without having to use her memory much at all. *Hail Mary, full of grace, the Lord is with thee. Blessed art thou among women, and blessed is the fruit of thy womb, Jesus. Holy Mary, Mother of God, pray for us sinners now, and at the hour of our death.* She repeated the prayer and repeated it again, silently, running the words over in her head without considering what they meant or why she had chosen this prayer in particular and gradually, like a kind of ether taking effect, the reason it was so important to do something in the first place wavered and blurred and Muriel's panic began to fade. She combed her fingers through her hair, patted it into place, let her gaze wander the room. Doodle's silver brush set on the bureau, her snow globe collection on a shelf. On a child-sized rocking chair in the corner sat a stuffed rabbit with a dozen strands of Mardi Gras beads wrapped around its neck and a pair of Muriel's old sunglasses perched on its brow. She could hear the faucet in the bathroom. There must have been a reason she'd turned it on. Most likely for Doodle's bath. That child was so easily distracted. She was probably puttering right now in Muriel's closet or at her vanity or in her jewelry box. She drew a breath to call her daughter's name, sighed it out, let her eyes drift shut. Her husband would be home soon and she was so tired all of a sudden. She'd just rest here a minute, not too long, then she would open her eyes and life would begin again.

Nora heard the back door open, Angus's keys clattering on the counter, water running in the kitchen sink. She figured he was rinsing dirty dishes before stowing them in the washer. A minute later, he poked his head into the den. With Murphy at her breast it was hard to notice much else about the world, but now that his father was here, she counted nine dirty diapers, seven wads of tissue, six half-empty glasses, three banana peels, and two baskets of unfolded laundry, all of it brought into high relief by the spotlight of her husband's gaze. These last few days, he'd been at the office more than he'd been home. She watched him wince at the mess, recover. He crossed the room and kissed both her and the baby on their respective brows.

"Rough morning?" he said, and though his tone was solicitous, Nora couldn't help hearing a backhanded insult in the words, as if the state of the room, the house, was evidence of her shortcomings.

"Fine," she said.

He brushed the hair back from her eyes.

"You stay put. I'll pick up."

Like she'd been about to drop the baby and spring to her feet. He hustled into the kitchen bearing diapers and banana peels, made another trip for the glasses and the tissues, then whisked back through in the other direction. "He smiled today," she said, but Angus didn't answer. She could hear him tidying in the bedroom, making the bed. When he returned, he'd changed into an old fishing shirt and worn-out jeans. Running shoes. He sat cross-legged on the floor and started folding laundry, his eyes on the TV. Satellite photos. Hurricane Raphael as seen from outer space.

"He smiled," she said again.

Angus beamed but even in that moment, she could tell he was distracted.

"A real smile," she said. "I smiled at him and he smiled back."

"I'm sorry I missed it," he said.

She dipped her chin to look at Murphy, eyes shut tight, mouth working, his fist balled against his cheek. What Angus couldn't understand was how he consumed her, not just her time but her consciousness. She didn't mind the mess. She hardly noticed. Angus was under the impression this was a rehashing of an argument they'd had when they got married. Nora refused to hire help because she wasn't the sort of woman who had a maid. Who cared if the house wasn't perfect all the time? And it was true. She did feel that way. But this was something else. There was a kind of power in her single-mindedness, purpose. Angus never second-guessed her but he let her know he felt left out, sighing and pouting around the house, and she couldn't altogether blame him. She had to remind herself sometimes to let him hold the baby, to listen when he spoke. Like now—his mouth was moving but it was like hearing him through a pane of glass.

"What?"

"I said Raphael looks like the real thing."

She watched Angus shake out a pillowcase, wrinkled from being left so long in the basket. It was clear that something was on his mind but it was too hard to puzzle through. He could just come out with it if he wanted her to know. He folded the pillowcase and set it on a stack of bedding.

"They're saying 120-mile-per-hour winds."

"It reminds me of a stain," she said.

He looked at her, eyebrows bunched up in a question.

"The satellite stuff. The pictures. They look like stains."

"There's something at the yard," he said.

He went on but Murphy pulled loose of her nipple while Angus spoke and it was about time to switch breasts anyway, so her attention was focused on making sure he had a proper latch. Her husband's voice was in the air but not something she was fully conscious of, like the white noise machine next to Murphy's bassinette. He was saying something about going back to work, a boat that needed his attention, and even as his words washed over her, half-absorbed, she knew she should be angry. He was talking about leaving her alone with their child during a hurricane. But she wasn't angry. In a strange way she felt relieved.

"What we'll do," he said, "is chart a course around the storm then come back after it's moved inland. I want you to go over to Momma's house. Or Doodle's. I'm not sure where they'll be."

"Can't somebody else take care of this?"

He stared at her a second, then went out into the foyer, rattled hangers in the closet there, returned wearing a raincoat. His hands were in his pockets.

"I need to do this myself," he said.

Doodle wanted to take a shower before walking over to her mother's house. After all, this hurricane was coming and she hadn't washed her hair last night and she might as well start off clean if she was going to have to rough it for a while. She stopped by Kathleen's room. Her oldest daughter was texting on her cell phone, stretched out on the bed, her feet propped against the wall, her head dangling off the side, hair draping toward the floor in a way that was particularly lovely to Doodle. Kathleen was sixteen, blonde, hair curly like her father's. Except she was going through a stage when she didn't like her curls. She wanted to look like everybody else, but Doodle knew the day would come when she'd be glad.

Her sister was reading a mystery novel on the floor at the foot of Kathleen's bed. Lucy, speaking of stages, was eleven years old, and spent most of her time following Kathleen around with a book, pretending she wasn't paying attention, wasn't memorizing every detail of Kathleen's walk, her mannerisms, her turns of phrase. Kathleen could be a handful but Doodle would always be grateful to her for allowing Lucy to hang around without having to be told. Once in a while Kathleen pretended to be annoyed, as if she felt some obligation, but Doodle had the idea that she secretly appreciated the audience, that she lived a great deal of her life performing for her sister as if her existence was being filmed.

Kathleen glared at Doodle upside down. "What?"

"We're going to Momma's for the hurricane."

"And?"

Kathleen kept staring until her mother backed out of the room.

Doodle took her time in the shower, flipped through a magazine while blow-drying her hair. Her given name was Deidre but her father had called her "Doodlebug" when she was a girl and her mother and her brothers had shortened it after a while. Fondly. The way families do. Her friends picked up on the nickname in school and it stuck because it suited her.

Kathleen was still texting when Doodle looked in again.

"I'm off to Momma's," she said.

Kathleen didn't bother to reply.

Lucy glanced up from her book. On the cover was a close-up of a woman's hand holding a martini glass filled with diamonds. Though you couldn't see beyond her wrist, somehow the image suggested that the rest of her was naked. *Murder is a Girl's Best Friend*.

"We'll be over in a minute, Mom."

"Right," Doodle said. "Okay."

Outside, a breeze sizzled through the boxwood and the hydrangea and Doodle's potted plants. She lowered herself into a wrought-iron chair on the patio and lit the single cigarette she allowed herself each day. Usually she waited until after dinner, smoked with a glass of wine or with a martini if her husband, Russell, was having one, but Russell was at an orthodontics conference in Chicago and she was spending the night with her mother. Only her husband and her daughters knew she still smoked and she'd sworn them to secrecy. Her mother thought it was tacky for a woman to smoke and her friends all thought she'd quit as a New Year's resolution.

The patio looked out over a wide expanse of lawn, the big magnolias, the mossy oaks. Her mother's great-grandfather had bought the property way back when this was still the country, before the rest of Mobile came seeping uphill from the river like a flood. First a few more houses. Then a school. Then the banks and the grocery chains. All the development was in place long before Doodle was born, but even as a girl, she'd had the sense of being marooned on a tranquil island in an ever-shifting sea of traffic and neighbors and barking dogs. Thirty acres. Right in the middle of town. Most days, the trees between the houses were teeming with cardinals and robins and wrens, the air musical with call and response, but now all she heard was quiet and she felt a tremor of anticipation. She knew it was absurd but she was excited about holing up with her mother and her daughters while a hurricane raged outside. She mashed the cigarette out and hurried across the lawn and up the back steps to her mother's house.

"Mom?"

Nothing.

"It's me, Mom."

No response.

She could hear water running upstairs, assumed her mother had had the same idea she did about cleaning up before the storm, and it pleased her to imagine the two of them thinking alike. She found a pitcher of iced tea in the refrigerator and poured herself a glass, considered calling Russell while she waited. She wanted him to know where he could find her during the storm. She sat at the kitchen table. The clock on the microwave said 10:24 AM. The table was situated beside a window and she surveyed her mother's view, measured it against her own, thought of her mother in this very spot on the mornings since her father died, her mother gazing out toward the land she'd saved for Percy.

The hired man, Dixon, kept those acres mowed, kept the shrubbery in check, but still Percy's lot looked down-at-heel, comparatively speaking, the grass mossy and threaded through with clover, dead limbs on living trees, leaves piled up under the magnolias, altogether lacking in design. She wondered, briefly, how closely her mother's expectations of her life reflected the end result but shook the thought away before it had a chance to gain real purchase and the thought wisped into the air above her head, where it hovered for a moment before dissolving, as if it had never crossed her mind. She looked at the clock again. 10:38. It occurred to her that the water she could hear was not running in the master bath, so she followed the sound through the dining room, past the mahogany table with hand-carved legs, vines and flowers twining up through the wood, past the matching sideboard and the secretary in which was kept her mother's wedding china. In the entry hall, a grandfather clock stood sentry by the door. From there, she went on up the stairs and creaked over the landing and found her mother in bed in the room of Doodle's childhood. Her hands were folded neatly in her lap.

"There you are," she said.

Her mother's eyes fluttered open and she smiled like she'd been in the middle of a pleasant dream.

Doodle saw, then, a finger of water crooking in from the bathroom and she felt the first inkling of fear, a faraway dawning that something wasn't right, but already her mind was working to rid itself of the notion.

"Did you fall asleep, Mom? Have you seen this mess?"

"It's time for your bath," her mother said.

Did she sound a little slurred? It was hard to hear over the water. Doodle waded in, twisted the taps. She pulled the plug and dried her hands.

"What are you talking about?" she said.

When her mother spoke again, her voice was faint. "Your father will be home soon," she said. "He'll want you kids ready for bed."

* * *

Angus pressed against the rail to let a Mexican kid go by. Maybe eighteen, nineteen, a length of extension cord coiled around his shoulder. He didn't nod or smile, just brushed past Angus like he wasn't even there, and Angus wondered if this kid had any idea what he was getting into. Double time might have sounded like good money but Angus would have bet double again whatever the kid would earn tonight that he had never been at sea in a blow like what was coming. Neither had Angus, to tell the truth, but he'd heard the stories from his father.

His phone buzzed in his pocket. Doodle. He was in no state of mind to deal with his sister. From this high up on the *Kagero*, he could look out over the warehouses and the dry docks and the slipways, all of it conjured into being by his father, all of it soon to be covered up with flood. A few steps shy of the wheelhouse, Angus heard a familiar voice and he hesitated at the open door, listened.

"So this fucking beaner, Regas, he wants to know can I come over to his place, says he's having trouble with the casero. He's gonna get evicted, right, and he can't work if he's got no place to live. I tell him I'm not his friend, I'm his jefe. But he's got his hat in his hands. I mean literally. He has no idea what he should do. So I say all right. I'll help him sort it out. But when I go over there, it's not an apartment, it's a fucking motel and they got fifteen people in the room. Sleeping in the tub at night and all over the floor and three or four to a bed. They're not even trying to hide it. There's this long row of shoes outside the door, work boots and sneakers and little old lady deals. It's no fucking wonder the manager wanted those people gone."

Angus stepped inside. Morris Peebles was perched in the captain's chair, a lit cigarette between his lips, his old face all wrinkles and weather damage, his eyebrows lifting at Angus's arrival, furrows of skin inching up and over his bald scalp like ripples in a pool.

"I'll be damned," he said.

He'd been holding forth to a second man, at least four decades his junior, who pinched the brim of his cap between thumb and forefinger, lifted it from his head and used the other three fingers to scratch the pale line of his part. Angus lowered himself onto a bench, tried to look like he was settling in.

"You thought I'd let you leave without me?"

Morris said, "Well."

Angus could feel the engine rumbling up through the hull into his spine. He felt it in his teeth, his hands. Bullard—that was the younger man's name. Morris's first mate.

"Dad would have wanted me here," Angus said.

"Your father," Bullard said, and then he bugged his eyes at Angus, his cap poised now over his chest. He didn't seem to know how to finish the thought. Almost a year since Angus's father died and still people went all solemn when he was mentioned. Finally, Bullard said, "I only met him a time or two but I was sorry as hell for you and your family."

"Now let's not get sentimental." Morris winked at Angus. "A.B. Ransom was an asshole just like his son. Exactly the sort of asshole who'd send us out into the middle of a fucking hurricane."

"There's no smoking in here, Morris," Angus said.

Morris laughed and stepped outside to flick the cigarette overboard and then somebody fuzzed in on the radio when he came back and suddenly everything was happening at once—lines cast off, the *Kagero* shuddering away from dock. Dozens of seagulls hovered over the bow. Angus pictured Nora and Murphy on the couch, the boy, his son, pulling loose of Nora's breast long enough to offer her his first true smile and he felt a weakening in his limbs. But it was too late for second thoughts. Up ahead, the river opened into Mobile Bay, the bank lined with marsh grass, coins of light reflected on the water. The light existed in shimmering patches until the *Kagero* got too close and then it vanished for an instant and reappeared an instant later, farther out in front, jittery and frail, less like something leading them than like a thing in flight.

Percy Ransom had always believed that he would outgrow masturbation, that a day would come

when he was beyond the reach of fantasy and desire, but here he was, thirty-eight years old, eyes
shut tight, sweat filming on his brow, holding in
mind a vision of his younger brother's wife. Not
two weeks before, he'd gone home for his nephew's
christening and caught a glimpse of Nora through
a half-open door at the reception, her breast as she
brought the baby to it, white skin, modest nipple,
head tilted in such a way as to drape her hair along
one cheek.

He pictured that hair, the exact same shade of
brown as Nora's eyes, shifting between her shoulder blades, imagined the sounds that she would
make. Despite the fact that he lived alone but for
his dog, he had, as always, locked himself in the
bathroom. His dog, Mutt, was a shepherd mix he'd
picked up in Montana and Percy didn't like the
way Mutt looked at him when he was jerking off.

He was panting hard, talking to himself, closing fast on climax when he heard someone calling
his name. His eyes popped open. He considered
ignoring the voice, but out here, this far from
nowhere, there was only one person it could be

and odds were Lester Hope knew he was home. Besides, if it was anyone other than Lester, Mutt would have barked.

"Hang on," Percy said.

He stowed his erection, took a minute to collect himself, then flushed to put Lester off the scent.

Horseshoe Bend had been his father's hunting camp, was Percy's now or would be when the paperwork was finished. He'd cut a deal with Angus to swap his interest in the shipyard for sole ownership of Horseshoe Bend. It was more complicated than that. Angus had brought the lawyers in, but Percy didn't care. He loved this place. The quiet. The river. The lean and looming pines.

They had almost a thousand acres up here, timbered enough to cover taxes and maintenance but not enough to affect the habitat, so the camp paid for itself while remaining more or less unchanged. The place was named for its position at a tapering curve in the Tombigbee River. One advantage of this location was that in winter the Tombigbee flooded the swamps at the neck of the horseshoe, driving deer and wild pigs onto the Ransoms' property and trapping them for the season. So many the woods couldn't feed them. You had to thin the population or they'd starve. Percy had visions of packing a deep freeze with venison and pork, living entirely off the land.

Already he'd planted a garden—tomatoes, cucumbers, peppers, beans. If he wasn't working in the garden, he spent his days spin-casting for largemouth, his evenings hiking logging trails to keep himself in shape, his nights studying up on canning vegetables or salting meat. He wanted nothing to pass his lips that he didn't have a hand in bringing to the table.

The lodge was built around a sort of great hall: vaulted ceilings buttressed by rough-cut beams, big stone hearth, plank floors worn to a high shine by sock-footed men, trophy bucks gazing glumly down from the walls. A pair of bunk rooms spoked off from there, one for the father, one for the sons, and there was a simple kitchen at the back of the house, and behind the kitchen a screened-in sleeping porch overlooking the river. He found Lester in the great hall, waiting in an old cane-bottom rocking chair, scratching Mutt just above his tail, which made the dog shiver and dance.

"Sister called," he said.

No cell reception at Horseshoe Bend and Percy's father had forbidden a landline, so if anybody needed to get in touch they called Lester, who delivered the message.

"Yeah?" Percy was surprised. He hadn't spoken with Doodle since the christening and even that was strained, half-hearted. Before that, the funeral. In between, silence. She disapproved, he understood, of his decision to cut his last ties to the shipyard. "What'd she want?"

"She say your momma took a fall."

He fished in his breast pocket, removed a scrap of paper. Doodle's number scribbled on the back of a hardware store receipt.

Percy said, "Is she hurt?"

Lester didn't answer right away. He'd been the caretaker at Horseshoe Bend for as long as Percy could remember, lived in a mobile home on the property with a Vietnamese woman he'd brought back like a souvenir from that war. Percy had always felt vaguely ridiculous in Lester's presence. At the moment, he couldn't shake the feeling that Lester knew what he'd been up to in the john.

Lester held Mutt's face in both hands, delivered his reply to the dog.

"You best come up to the house," he said.

It took a minute, standing in the exact middle of the waiting room and clutching her purse with both hands, for Doodle to realize that she was not alone. A uniformed police officer was sitting quietly in a chair to Doodle's right. Female. Black. Details that surprised Doodle for no good reason. Like the woman was wearing a police costume. Her legs were crossed like a man's, her uniform hat hung on her knee, her eyes intent on the TV mounted on the wall, a reporter in Bienville Square murmuring on about the coming storm. The policewoman was pretty, or she might have been if she hadn't looked so stern.

Doodle lowered herself into a chair and tried to remember what the duty nurse had told her about her mother's condition but she couldn't concentrate, couldn't stop seeing her mother in bed, that faraway expression on her face. And what she'd said. That was the worst thing. "Your father will be home soon." There had passed a moment after hearing her mother's words when Doodle felt lifted outside of time. The past was not the past and she was still a girl, putting off bath time because bath time meant bedtime close upon its heels, and her father really would be home within the hour. Then her mother had shut her eyes and refused to open them again.

Doodle fished her phone from her purse but the battery was dead. That was so exactly like her it made her grit her teeth. She'd already left voice mails for Angus, both at home and on his cell, left a message for Percy with the caretaker up at Horseshoe Bend, and she wanted to try Russell again at the hotel. He had no idea what was happening, she knew that, but she couldn't help feeling angry that he'd abandoned her to deal with this alone.

Her father had never entirely approved of Russell, not because he didn't like him—everybody liked Russell—but because he was terrified of dentists. Technically, Russell was an orthodontist but her father lumped anyone who chose to work with their hands in other people's mouths into a single, sadistic bunch. He was so terrified, in fact, that before Doodle was born, before he married her mother, he'd felt the ache of a cavity and instead of having it filled, he'd gone from dentist to dentist until he found someone unscrupulous enough to pull his teeth. All of them. One final, terrible agony, so he'd never have to sit in a dentist's chair again. Some of her most vivid memories from childhood: her father with his dentures removed, his mouth collapsed like an old man's in a young, otherwise handsome face. The sound he made sucking on his dentures when he was lost in thought. The dentures themselves, like a prop, in a glass beside his bed. What he'd done had seemed more brave than ridiculous to Doodle when she was a girl.

A nurse appeared in the doorway with a doctor at her side and Doodle straightened up in case they were looking for her. She dropped the phone into her purse, lifted the purse into her lap. But the nurse pointed the doctor in the direction of the policewoman—relief flooded Doodle—and he crossed the room, wiping his hands on the backs of his scrubs. You could tell from his expression that he had no good news to give her.

"Officer Pruitt?" the doctor said, and Officer Pruitt stood.

Doodle inventoried her purse to keep from staring: phone, lipstick, Kleenex, hand sanitizer, wallet, hairbrush, Visa bill, Amex bill—she was hiding these from Russell—and a permission slip for Lucy's school that she kept meaning to sign.

When the doctor spoke again, his voice was so soft that Doodle couldn't make out his words, but Officer Pruitt said, "Don't you tell me that."

Doodle didn't want to hear the rest. She pushed to her feet, found her way back to the nurse's station. Someone new was manning the desk. The phone was ringing and the nurse held up a finger for Doodle to be patient while she took the call. "I don't know," she said. "I just came on. All right. I'll tell him if I see him." She hung up, sighed, turned her attention to Doodle. "What can I do for you?" she said.

Muriel gasped awake from a dream of forgetfulness and water. She was alone in bed. Angus was crying in the bassinette but she had a sense, nothing more, that it wasn't him who woke her, that whatever had called her up from sleep had roused her son as well. She couldn't be sure if the alarm clanging through her was a response to this sensation or to some vague, edgy residue of her dream. She clutched the blanket to her chest and listened for her husband, heard a chair scrape on the balcony, a cough. Reassured, she went to comfort Angus. The clock on the nightstand said half past one. It wasn't time yet for his bottle. She was rocking him in the glider, calming herself as much as him, when she heard a door close in the kitchen.

There were two stairwells in the house, one leading from the back hall to the landing outside Doodle's room, the other from the front door to a landing that separated the master suite from Percy's room, the room Angus would share as soon as Muriel was ready to let him go. That's where she was headed, inhaling the baby's scent as she crossed the landing to look in on his brother, but even the smell of him wasn't enough to put her at ease. The door to the balcony was ajar, cigarette smoke and winter seeping in. She found Percy balled up on the mattress, knees tucked under his chest, elbows pulled in close, face mashed nose-first into the pillow like he was attempting to burrow deeper into his dreams. She covered him, then stepped out onto the balcony.

A.B. had his feet propped up on the wrought-iron table, highball glass in one hand, cigarette in the other. Muriel was blessed with a gift for slumber. She looked forward to it, had been known, when she was young, to embark on daylong voyages of sleep. She took comfort in the act of shutting her eyes and leaving the world behind. Her husband was not so lucky. He swore that he was incapable of falling asleep until he quite literally couldn't keep his eyes open one minute longer, swore that if he tried, worry would crank his mind up and he couldn't make it stop. Most nights, no matter the weather, he would kiss her goodnight and adjourn to the balcony where he waited for exhaustion to befall him. Often as not, he never made it into bed. She'd find him still out there in the morning, head resting on his arms like a schoolboy dozing at his desk.

He didn't notice her watching him, her shadow leaning toward him from the door. He appeared so perfectly within himself, she was tempted to leave him be, but she remembered the door closing downstairs, an ordinary sound made menacing by the hour.

"Did you hear something?" she whispered.

As if the act required effort, he turned, dropped his feet to the floor. The ice rattled in his glass. With a warmth at odds with his rough voice, he said, "Hey, little mother. How's my little man?"

Light from the landing tangled up in his smoke.

"I heard something in the kitchen," she said.

"Percy?"

"He's in bed. I looked."

"What about Doodle?"

"You look," she said. "I don't want to go by myself."

Muriel could almost see him deciding that this was something womanish, his tired wife hearing noises in the middle of the night, nothing to worry about. He stood and touched her shoulder and she could smell the whiskey on him as he passed. She followed him back through their bedroom and out onto the other landing, moving now toward Doodle's room. Muriel hoped it wasn't Doodle. She had been in the middle of a tantrum when A.B. got home from work and he was not pleased, and Muriel worried that if she was out of bed now without permission, he'd lose his temper. His hand was on the knob when they heard cabinets opening and closing in the kitchen, water running in the sink. Doodle couldn't reach the cabinets. A.B. hesitated, peeked in her room just to be sure.

When he turned back to Muriel, he brought a finger to his lips and mouthed, "Stay here."

Angus had dozed off in her arms and she hugged him to her while A.B. slipped back into the bedroom. He returned holding the pistol he kept hidden in a lockbox in the closet.

He shouted, "Is somebody in my house?"

A moment later came the answer. "Yes." That one word, matter-of-fact, reasonable, thoroughly unintimidated. A man's voice. Something about its lack of emotion made her heart race in her chest.

"Well, who is it?" A.B. said.

There passed a few seconds of silence—Muriel felt it stretching out, her heart reacting, pounding, like the quiet was a drug—as if whoever was in the kitchen was considering his reply.

"It's me," the voice said at last.

"Are you robbing me, cocksucker?"

The voice said, "I don't know."

A.B. looked at her. She didn't know what she was seeing in his face. Then he made sure the pistol was loaded. Then he crept on down the stairs.

He knew Babydoll would be watching one of her programs in the den, so Lester took Percy around back, let him in through the kitchen, left him alone to make his call. The trailer was spotless, reeked of bleach. Babydoll liked to stay ahead of a mess and there wasn't much for her to do in the woods except clean house and work in her garden. That and look at the TV. She never acted like she minded, though. She didn't know anything else, to tell the truth, and no doubt this was better than what she'd had growing up in Vietnam. Which was nothing. Dirt floors. Rice and cabbage. Bowel movements in a field. And he was always buying her new things. Like that home theater system taking up most of the den. Screen big as the hood of his truck. Lester had installed the satellite himself.

He went in there now, cupped his hand over the top of her head and she leaned into his palm without looking away from the screen. She was so small he had to order her clothes from children's catalogs.

"We got company," he said.

She chattered at him. Babydoll understood more English than she spoke and Lester spoke more Vietnamese than he understood but he always managed to get her drift, which in this case was, why didn't those people get a phone so they wouldn't have to be coming around to her house, tracking dirt in on her floors?

He dropped his hands to her shoulders, massaged the way she liked, kissed the part in her hair.

"Fix the man something to drink."

He took her place on the couch when she was gone, switched channels. He wanted to check in on the hurricane. Likely it would make some noise up here. They had a man stationed on the street in downtown Mobile. Not much weather yet but the man said landfall sooner than expected. Hurricane Raphael had picked up speed. He was switching back to Babydoll's program just as Percy came into the room.

"What's the word?"

"No answer." Percy sipped from a glass of water and pointed at the TV. "That's some rig," he said.

Lester said, "Three hundred eighteen channels."

"Did you know," Percy said, "that the first communications satellite launched into orbit from this country was owned by Western Union?"

Lester looked at him a second.

"About when was that?"

Percy shrugged. "The seventies."

"Still not much on, though," Lester said.

Percy rolled the water glass across his brow. Lester had already told him everything he knew. Which wasn't much. His mother had fallen. They'd taken her to the hospital in an ambulance. He thought it best not to describe the way his sister sounded on the phone. Babydoll was leaning in the doorway behind them and when Percy set his glass on the coffee table, she started jabbering at his back. Percy looked to Lester for translation. He didn't know for sure but he would have bet she was telling him to use a coaster. There was a coaster right there in plain sight.

"She say we'll listen for the phone. If Sister calls again, I'll come get you."

He moved Percy's glass to the coaster himself. Percy didn't notice. He was worried. You could see that. Nodding and blinking like Lester had dragged him out of bed.

*   *   *

Lucy re-read the last line of her book—*The man in black walked away in the rain, Esmerelda's diamonds clicking in his pocket*—but the ending wasn't anymore satisfying than the first time. She felt weird, disoriented. Then she realized it was raining for real, the windows of her sister's room blurred with run-off, the sound of it all around her. Her mother had left them with strict instructions: go immediately to Uncle Angus's, explain the situation to Aunt Nora, ride out the storm over there unless she called. Lucy wasn't sure how much time had passed since then but it was enough to finish her book and here she was still in her sister's room, Kathleen murmuring now into the phone.

"I'm not sure that's a good idea," Kathleen said, but her voice was flirty and shrewd. She was talking to Dexter King. He lived just down the road. Kathleen snuck out at least three nights a week to meet Dexter at the empty lot, Uncle Percy's lot, and Lucy followed her sometimes. They hid themselves inside a huge magnolia so what went on between them was hard to see, but Lucy could hear her sister's voice, telling Dexter where to put his hands, his lips. The silence between those moments was profound.

Sometimes, by daylight, she returned to the magnolia and parted the branches and stepped inside. That's what it was like. Moving from outside in. The magnolia was at least three stories tall and beneath its canopy was a cool, shadowy space big enough to stand in, big enough to move around, the world and the sky barely visible through the leaves.

"It does sound beautiful," Kathleen said.

She turned on her side to face the wall and said something else that Lucy couldn't hear. Rain drummed on the roof. Not the hurricane yet, Lucy didn't think, just some lesser storm blown ashore like a herald before a king.

"We need to go," Lucy said. "Mom'll kill us."

Kathleen rolled her eyes, covered the phone with her hand.

"Evaporate," she said, and Lucy headed down the hall to her room carrying *Murder is a Girl's*

Best Friend. For a while, she stretched out in bed listening to the rain and trying to get caught up in worrying about her grandmother, pictured her in a gloomy room, machines beeping and purring, her mother beside the bed wracked with despair, tried to make herself cry but it felt like her grandfather's funeral, the sight of him in his coffin, waxy and pale, as hard to believe in as a trashy novel.

Lucy had seen her grandfather not an hour before he died, maybe less, she wasn't sure. For all she knew she was the last person to see him alive. She'd been out on the lawn that morning chasing a butterfly. She had the idea that she would catch it and bring it to school for Mrs. Curtis, who taught science and kept a collection of specimens in a glass-front case. But the butterfly was flitting way up in a dogwood and she couldn't reach it and the tree was too delicate to climb. It was early enough that there was still dew on the grass. Her grandfather must have seen her as he was leaving for the shipyard.

"Hello, Little Girl," he said, and she said, "Hey, Big Man," because that's what they called each other, just the two of them.

He asked what she was doing and she told him and he took off his panama hat and reached up into the tree and scooped the butterfly down to her. She liked that her grandfather was the last man in the world who wore a hat to work.

"I'll bring it right back," she said, already dashing for the house, holding the hat against her chest to keep the butterfly from escaping. "Let me put him in a jar."

"I'll get it later," he said. "I'm in a hurry," and then his heart attacked him on the way to work and he ran off the road and died.

She still had the hat, kept it hidden under her bed. Pale straw. Black band. Not even Kathleen knew. Lucy lay on her belly and reached way back to the wall to find it. She dusted it off and put it on and tipped the brim back from her eyes. Tiptoed down the hall and eavesdropped outside her sister's room.

"How will I know?" Kathleen said into the phone.

Rain clattered against the window like a summons, like someone was pitching handfuls at the pane.

The doctor rapped once on the open door, then stepped inside without waiting for an invitation and introduced herself to Doodle. She checked her mother's IV. Checked the ventilator. Made a notation on her mother's chart. She wore her hair in a messy topknot. Eyeglasses with neon-yellow frames. Doodle had failed to catch her name. She wasn't sure how much time had passed since they moved her mother out of surgery and into the ICU. The doctor leaned on the windowsill and crossed her arms and Doodle took her mother's hand.

"We did the best we could but you need to understand your mom's hurt pretty bad." There was a veneer of practiced sympathy in the doctor's tone, an affected folksiness. She went on, using words like hemorrhage and hippocampus. Doodle listened without hearing in a chair beside her mother's bed. She understood that she needed to pay attention, ask questions, gather facts for her brothers, but not breaking down required all her concentration. The doctor turned her head and tapped the base of her own skull—she was explaining something to Doodle—and Doodle noticed that the back of her neck was paler than her face.

"I tried to call my brothers," Doodle said. "They need to hear this."

The doctor paused, the ventilator wheezing into the silence between them. Doodle felt a prickle rising in her cheeks. When Doodle said nothing more, the doctor pressed ahead.

"The likelihood is some damage has already been done so even if she responds—and I'm not ruling that out—but even if she does you're gonna have to make some hard decisions pretty soon."

"My husband is out of town," Doodle said. "My father died last year. My brothers. I can't do this alone."

She knew how she must have sounded to this woman but she couldn't help herself. When her father died, Angus had made every decision, handled every last detail. Doodle's role had been to hold her mother's hand, to break the news gently to her children, to help Percy pick out a tie and smile through her tears in the receiving line and make sure everyone had a drink or plate of hors d'oeuvres during the wake. She could do those things. She could not do this. Behind the doctor, rain streaked the window glass but this side of the building was sheltered by a courtyard, the window double-paned and inlaid with mesh, thick enough that you could barely hear the wind.

"This is a lot to take in," the doctor said, "I understand," though it was clear to Doodle that this woman found her pathetic. "I'll come check on you in a while."

Then she went out and Doodle was alone again with her mother. Her head was wrapped in gauze, lips parted, though no air was moving through them. The ventilator inflated and deflated her lungs. Despite all that, she still looked like herself, her eyelids fluttering, her face aware. Of something but not this: this white room, the rain against the window, her daughter right here beside the bed.

The sound of the gunshot woke all three children at once but Muriel ignored their cries and went dashing down the stairs, Angus wailing in her arms, visions of her husband lying shot and bleeding on the kitchen floor playing in her head. She found him with the gun at his side, a dizzy look on his face, like he was on the verge of being sick. Facing him was a young white man with his hands in the air. He was wearing a mink coat, her mink coat she realized after a moment, his long arms jutting from the sleeves, his exposed wrists thin and fragile-looking. The air smelled like fireworks. The floor was littered with broken glass.

"I might have killed you," A.B. said.

He brought his free hand up to his chest, took a breath, then closed the distance between himself and the young man in one long stride and hit him backhanded across the face. The young man crumpled, brought his elbows and knees up to protect himself.

"You stupid, crazy fucker," A.B. said.

Angus was still crying and now Doodle was out of bed, calling from the head of the stairs, and all of this was so far removed from what Muriel had expected, that she felt disoriented, lightheaded with confusion and relief. Her eyes found the bullet hole in the wall, a perfect black circle surrounded by crumbling plaster, and it occurred to her that A.B. had pulled his shot on purpose. She identified the shards on the floor as the remains of a juice glass from the cabinet over the sink. A.B. was extending his hand to help the young man up. The young man whimpered and flinched and A.B. had to swat his arms aside in order to pull him to his feet. She studied his face more closely, recognition creeping over her. Mitchell King. Ted and Margaret's boy. The one who'd gone to special schools. The one who still lived with his parents, though he was more than old enough to be out on his own. Rumor had followed him through his adolescence. The fire in the Caldwells' garage. The Pressmans' missing cat. Nothing ever proved or disproved. The Kings hardly mentioned him anymore and no one ever asked.

A.B. walked him over to a chair at the breakfast table now and forced him to sit. He took the opposite chair, lit a cigarette with a kitchen match, offered one to Mitchell, who accepted it with trembling hands. His fingers were bumping so vigorously he couldn't strike a match. A.B. took the cigarette, lit it with his own, then passed it back.

"What's the matter with you?" he said.

"I was cold," Mitchell said. "I was thirsty."

"Do you know where you are?"

Mitchell's eyes, Muriel noticed, were almost imperceptibly crossed and so wide open at that moment he looked like one of Doodle's dolls. He glanced from A.B. to Muriel, then settled his gaze on Angus, who was wailing hard and loud enough that he couldn't catch his breath.

To Muriel, A.B. said, "Hush that baby up. And see to Doodle and Percy. They're likely scared to death."

The heat in his words returned Muriel to herself and she bounced Angus in her arms on the way back upstairs. There was Doodle on the landing, all keyed up and afraid, and here was Percy whimpering toward her from his room. She murmured reassurances, let them climb into her bed, joined them with the baby. In a little while, A.B. would recount the details for her, how Mitchell had woken up in their backyard with no idea where he was or how he'd gotten there, how the back door was unlocked, how he'd found her mink in the hall closet and fixed himself a glass of water. But that was later. Now, she lifted her purse from the nightstand and fished her rosary out and handed it to Doodle, let the beads pool in the cup of her daughter's palms. The rosary was knit of silver and pearls, handed down by Muriel's mother, and Doodle looked upon it with dual reverence. She was seven years old, a second grader at Saint Ignatius School, at an age when piety held a certain glamour for a certain kind of child. She was also, Muriel knew, an ordinary little girl, in love with pretty things and the rosary was a favorite accessory in her dress-up games.

"Will you say it with me?"

Doodle said, "They haven't taught us yet," so Muriel walked her through the prayers, the sign of the cross, the Apostles' Creed, an Our Father on the first large bead, Hail Marys on the three small beads that followed. *Hail Mary, full of grace, the Lord is with thee.* Angus dozed off almost right away in the crook of Muriel's arm. She worried that Percy, who was only four, would grow restless with the rosary but he seemed to sense that something out of the ordinary had happened in their house tonight, was happening still right there in the bedroom. Perhaps it was simply the fact that it was so late and they were all awake and he had been granted the rare privilege of his parents' bed, but he leaned his head on Muriel's shoulder and chimed, "Amen," when Doodle and Muriel finished another prayer. Glory Be to the Father on the next large bead, then ten Hail Marys on the adjacent beads, and so on through a final sign of the cross and Muriel found herself, despite everything, lulled calm by the prayers and the nearness of her children and the faraway murmur of her husband's voice bubbling up through the floor.

The longer he let himself dwell on the nature of Doodle's call, the more afraid Percy became. She wouldn't have bothered if whatever had happened to their mother wasn't serious. If this was an emergency, he wanted to be home. He drank rum and Dr Pepper and paced the lodge, waiting for a report from Lester. Mutt trailed him at first, back and forth, back and forth, nails ticking on the hardwood, but the dog got bored after a while and sprawled on the rug, his head turning to follow Percy. Finally, when Percy couldn't stand not knowing another minute, he freshened his drink and whistled Mutt into the passenger seat of his truck.

For half an hour, the road itself was enough to occupy his thoughts but by the time he reached French Camp, came coasting to a stop at the town's only light, the bait shop and the post office, the barbecue joint, the flea market, the little high school set back from the road, all of them dark now, not another car in sight, worry about his mother had begun to creep back in. He thought of her alone in that big old house. Doodle and Angus were right next door and he was glad for that, grateful even, but they couldn't be with her all the time and he doubted their proximity made the nights any easier since his father died. How quiet the house must have seemed, how empty. His father could take up space like nobody in the world. In that moment, he was sure of two things: first, that her loneliness was incurable except by time, and second, that its incurability was beside the point. He knew what she wanted, what he might have done. Her windows looked out over the lawn to the lot she'd saved for him. How hard would it have been to build a little house back there, meet a girl, live a life?

"Harder than it sounds," he told Mutt, who was hanging his head out the window.

Percy had always felt the pull of expectation, the shipyard, the empty lot, and he half believed that one day some latent switch would throw itself inside his chest, some gear would finally catch, and he'd desire the very life he'd been resisting. He'd run a charter boat out of Nags Head for a while. Bought a drive-in movie theater in Pigeon Forge. Opened a bar in Bozeman, which he called Blue Sky after the Allman Brothers' song and not, as many of his customers believed, after the ubiquitous firmament of the West. He lived in a little apartment upstairs. During the day, Mutt lounged in the open door or wandered between the tables begging scraps and at night, when Percy brought a woman home, he tried to nose between them in the bed.

Then Angus called to tell him that their father was gone. Heart attack. Hard to imagine that something so ordinary could kill his father. When they hung up, Percy said, "You ever been to Alabama?"

The woman in his bed said, "Why on earth would anybody want to go to Alabama?" She was round-hipped and heavy-breasted, dark roots visible in her blonde hair. Her husband drove a long-haul truck.

"I was talking to the dog," he said.

He met the rain ten miles farther down the road. Nothing serious at first but he pulled Mutt inside and rolled the window up. It occurred to Percy that he hadn't seen anybody headed his way in quite some time.

Another twenty miles and the gas gauge was brushing empty but the next three stations he passed were closed. He was getting nervous when he saw lights maybe fifty yards ahead, made glittery and indistinct by rain. A woman was locking the doors as Percy pulled into the lot. She hesitated, then waved and opened the doors again and Percy rolled up to the pump.

When the tank was full, he left Mutt to guard the truck and dashed inside.

"Damn," he said, meaning the rain.

The woman was waiting behind the counter. A birthmark ran from her chin to the lower lid of her left eye. Like a dialogue bubble in a comic book. It made her look naïve somehow.

"Tell me about it. I figured on a big night with all these people clearing out of Mobile but now

I'm thinking it's not worth it. Hole up. Stay dry. That's what I'm talking about."

Percy headed for the coffee machine but it was already washed and shut down for the night. He was tired enough and tipsy enough that more booze was the only thing other than coffee likely to keep him awake. He was on his way to grab a six-pack, when he realized what he'd just heard.

"Clearing out?" he said.

The woman squinted at him, then smiled, like Percy was pulling her leg. Twirled a ring of car keys on her finger.

"Seriously," Percy said.

Another appraisal—the squint, the smile. "There's a hurricane coming, mister." She gestured at the night, the storm, the world out there. "Where you been?"

According to the barometer, air pressure had dropped three millibars in the last hour, which meant the eye was roughly a hundred miles to port, the *Kagero* lifting and falling on the swells, lifting and slowly falling again, sickness rising in Angus by the minute, washing over him entire, weakness in his knees and elbows and prickling on the insides of his cheeks, wind battering the wheelhouse like it wanted in out of the rain.

"Your old man would've loved this shit," Morris said. "I remember we built a yacht for this oil man back in the nineties, Threadgil, he had all these rigs out in the Gulf. Your dad hated that sonofabitch. He was always complaining and making last-minute demands and the oil business was in the tank or so he said, kept trying to pay less than he owed. But somehow he had plenty of money for this big party for the launch. Band and caterers and shit. Anyhow, your dad had me go out looking for a storm on the maiden voyage." He laughed and shook his head. "I found one, too. I mean a doozy. Women in party dresses puking in every corner."

As if on cue, Angus's stomach boiled up into his throat. He was too preoccupied by his symptoms, by the effort of resisting their inevitable finale, to know if Morris was having fun at his expense or just telling stories. His father had taught him to focus on the horizon—no matter how much a boat rocked and dove and rose and plunged, the horizon was always steady—but the world beyond the wheelhouse was a blur of rain and mist sheared from the waves, everything white out there, no horizon to focus on, no form or shape, like they were passing through a cloud, so that when a cargo hatch was torn loose from the bow and borne aloft by wind, it was visible only for an instant, unidentifiable in the storm, a shadow swooping close enough to the bridge that Angus flinched, then on through the cluster of antennae on the roof, leaving the radar dark.

"The hell was that?" he said.

"Hatch," Morris said, "if I had to guess."

Angus gestured at the vacant radar screens, worried that if he opened his mouth again he wouldn't be able to control what might come out.

"That's not the problem," Bullard said.

The seasickness made it difficult to concentrate and it took Angus a moment to catch on. Swells were washing over the deck, which meant without a hatch they'd start taking on water in the hold.

Not a desperate concern in and of itself. Took a lot of water to drown a boat this big. But some- one would have to go below and seal the doors between holds or the pumps could fall behind and the rest of the *Kagero* could be flooded.

"I'll go," Angus said.

The last thing he wanted was to vomit in front of Morris. Morris studied him for a second, then shrugged and slapped a flashlight into his palm and pointed at a life vest in the corner.

"I'm not sure that's a good idea," Bullard said, but Angus was too sick to be offended or afraid.

"He'll be fine," Morris said. He squinted and bunched his lips. After a moment, he said to Angus, "Maybe Bullard's got a point. Don't try to seal the holds yourself. Get one of the deckhands to do it. How's your Spanish?"

"So-so."

"Find Ramirez. His English is pretty decent."

Angus nodded and clanged down a set of per- forated metal stairs, then along a corridor, brac- ing himself against the wall as the floor lurched and sagged beneath his feet, his brain lurching in his skull. Ahead, he could see a pale oblong of light from the mess hall and he could hear voices but all the talking was in Spanish. He found five deckhands holding hands around a metal table as if conducting a séance. They were all wearing life jackets. One had a bucket between his knees. The sight of the bucket and the thought of what was in it brought the sickness up but Angus managed to choke it down.

"Este barco esta embrujado por un fantasma solitario," one of the men said.

Angus looked at their faces, pallid with fear, but he didn't know which one had spoken until he spoke again. The one with a crucifix on a chain hanging outside his T-shirt. Angus had heard the word for ship. About the rest he had no idea.

"Podemos oírlo," the man said. "Vive en las entrañas del barco. Todos nos vamos a morir."

The word for live. The word for die. The word for ship again.

"Just stay put," he said.

He followed the corridor to a second set of stairs. Halfway down, he opened his mouth and leaned over the railing and let it out. The sound he made seemed far removed from his own throat. His vomit swirled in the water in the corridor. Already inches deep. Giving in to the nausea only made it worse. He was light-headed with it, his spine filled up with sand.

At the bottom of the stairs, he heard more voices. English this time. The engine room was aft of him. He waited a second to see if anyone emerged, if anyone had heard him, then pressed forward to the first cargo hold. The door was open, latched against the wall, wind whistling through like breath over a bottle magnified a thousand times.

He followed his flashlight through the first hold and into the second, steel beams bracing the walls like ribs, and there he dropped onto his hands and knees and vomited again, emptied himself into the water. It didn't help. His eyeballs swayed in their sockets. His head wobbled on his neck. The water rolled over his wrists. He'd been seasick before but nothing like this. This was phantasmagoric. This was vast.

The wind died down a moment, as if catching its own breath, and in the sudden quiet, he would have sworn he heard a flapping noise, like shuffling cards, accompanied by a rasping voice. "I'm so alone," it said. Not quite human. Part of him knew he was being overdramatic but another part, the part wobbling and quivering inside his skin, believed that he was hearing the voice of his own regret. He knew this night was a mistake. The storm would bring them down or worse, the ship would pass the storm intact but something terrible would happen to his wife and son while he was gone. He curled into a ball and worked backward over the last few months, the way it seemed he'd lost his wife to motherhood, this new and inexplicable distance between them, and from there to Murphy's birth, how he'd tried to be a good husband, a good father, how he'd cut Murphy's umbilical cord, something his own father never would have done, how he'd held Nora's hand, coached and encouraged her, the way he'd been taught in birthing class, how he felt like an appendage, a distraction, how during her

pregnancy he'd had the sense that she was bur-
rowing into herself, as if into her own womb. He
slipped down his memory to the months they'd
had in the new house before she got pregnant,
Sunday afternoons in bed, the secret places on
her body, all the way back to the day they met,
that wedding in New Orleans. The bride was the
daughter of a client whose company ran cargo
barges on the Mississippi. Nora was waitress-
ing for the caterer, making pocket money while
she finished at Tulane. She was tall, fair, her hair
impossibly soft-looking as it brushed across
her back, her cheeks flushed from the heat. The
black skirt. The crisp white blouse. The way she
shouldered her tray. No makeup. He hadn't been
able to find a date and he was bored, made lonely
by too much wine, wound up following Nora
through the reception, putting himself in her
path, obliging her to offer him hors d'oeuvres.
Finally, as he was selecting a canapé from her
tray, she said, "Ask."

"Oh," he said, and he could feel the heat rising
in his face. "May I please have a canapé?"

Nora smiled and rolled her eyes. "My name?" she said. "My number? Whatever. Tell me that I'm beautiful."

And so he did.

"How do you feel?"

"I'm not sure," he said.

"I was just thinking that now, when I tell you to please leave me alone, you won't feel like I'm the one that got away or something. Like you missed a chance. If only you'd had the courage to speak to me, et cetera. I thought maybe you'd feel relieved."

"I see."

"And?"

"It's complicated. I'm embarrassed. That's one thing. There are other things, too, though they're harder to describe. None of them feel like relief. Maybe that'll kick in down the road. Years from now I'll be in bed with my soon-to-be ex-wife, wondering where everything went wrong, and I'll remember this moment and take comfort in the fact that you humiliated me. I have my doubts but you never know."

Nora looked at him a second.

"I'm so alone," she said, but he knew those weren't her words. His regret was intruding even upon his memory. Nora had asked him for a pen at that point, given him her number after all. Nine weeks later they were married.

Angus gathered himself and struggled to his feet and the *Kagero* fell away beneath him, plunging for what felt like a long time. He stumbled toward the last door just as the boat began to rise, water pouring through between the holds, enough to sweep his legs from under him, to wash him backward along the floor, enough to leave him beached and gasping against the wall. The wind was all around him now, filling his ears like liquid, and as the *Kagero* dipped again, he saw what looked like a gilded cage bobbing toward the foremost hold. It disappeared over the sill and he was almost sure he had imagined it, or if he hadn't that it would be lifted up and away and overboard through the ruined hatch, but as they climbed again, here it came, rushing back over the sill and into his arms.

There, before his eyes was a great, black bird with a long, yellow beak, the very demon of his regret, his mistake given essence and form.

The bird shivered water from its feathers.

"I'm so alone," it said.

Her mother had a seizure not long after midnight, legs jittering beneath the sheet, hips bucking, hands balled into fists, eyes squeezed shut, her mouth drawn into an awful smile. The nurses came rushing in. A doctor Doodle hadn't met before explained that this was to be expected, given her mother's condition. It was like a short, he said. The blood on her mother's brain. It was like pouring water on a hard drive. Those were his exact words. Doodle wanted to scratch his eyes.

She couldn't stand that room another minute, couldn't wait around for another seizure, couldn't bear the thought of seeing her mother like that again. The power had been out almost an hour, the generators reserved for necessities, the corridor thick with patients from the windward side of the building, displaced in case the hurricane got the better of the windows, nurses bustling between the beds, the hospital lit only by the glow of apparatus, a pale and greenish glow like a sickly cousin of true light.

Through occasional open doors, Doodle could see that most of the rooms on her mother's side were doubled or tripled-up but no one had even asked about sharing her mother's room. Doodle didn't know if that was because of her condition, how serious it was, how hopeless, and this idea made her afraid, though it was difficult to imagine being more afraid than she already was. Surely there were limits to the body's capacity for fear. For everything. That's what glands were for, she thought. Some gland somewhere woke up at the last minute and released a haze of chemicals into your blood. She wondered about her mother. Her face was peaceful enough in repose, eyes darting back and forth under their lids like she was dreaming, but during the seizure, there was something very much like fear present in her features. That or pain. The doctor had assured Doodle that it was all reflex, electrical misfiring, that she didn't feel a thing, but if that was true, her mother was lost and Doodle wanted more than anything to leave that possibility behind, find her way back to the lobby and out to her car, wanted to keep driving until Russell or Angus or even Percy had sorted all this out, wanted to rush home and wrap her daughters in her arms, but she was hemmed in by the storm and no one was coming and she couldn't have left her mother regardless. She knew that. For now, she would settle for putting a little distance between herself and where she'd been.

She pressed the button for the elevator, waited, pressed it again before remembering that there was no power. Blushed. She found the stairwell around the corner, a rolled-up magazine wedged under the door to keep it open. Red emergency bulbs on the stairs. Two floors down, she thought she smelled cigarette smoke, barely perceptible, like a memory of smoke or an olfactory hallucination brought on by her own craving. These days, it was hard to imagine anybody crass enough or desperate enough to light up in a hospital but the odor kept growing stronger as she descended. Finally, in the basement, she found the police officer from the waiting room sitting on the floor with her back against the wall. Officer Pruitt. Her head was tipped back and she glared at Doodle, down her nose and through a cloud of smoke, as if daring Doodle to tell her to put it out.

"Can I bum one of those?" Doodle said.

Officer Pruitt eyed her a second longer, then lifted her hips to scrounge a pack from the pocket of her trousers. She tapped out a wrinkled cigarette, passed Doodle a lighter.

"I haven't smoked since I started the academy. Going on four years now. Paid an orderly ten bucks for what was left in his pack."

"I've been trying to quit myself," Doodle said.

She sat on the steps, lit her cigarette, returned the lighter. That first inhale was exquisite. It had been so long since her last cigarette that this one dizzied her a little. Officer Pruitt tipped her head in the direction of a windowless, metal door, the word *MORGUE* stenciled there in chipped black letters.

"Nobody down here worried about our smoke," she said.

"I guess not."

"My partner's in there." She inhaled, exhaled. The smoke hung low between them. "Got himself run over during a traffic stop. Right up on Dauphin Street. He's at the window writing a ticket when this kid drives by looking at his phone."

"My mother slipped in the bathroom," Doodle said.

To Doodle's amazement, she felt absolutely nothing at these words. She waited, sounding her depths for a rush of emotion that was surely coming, but she was perfectly still inside.

"This place ought to be full of cops," Officer Pruitt said. "It would be, too, if not for this hurricane. Everybody loved Hildebran."

She lit another cigarette off the ember of the first, then mashed the first one out on the bottom of her shoe. Doodle considered mentioning her brothers, her husband, how she, too, was all alone. But it didn't matter. So many stupid ways to live and die. She felt a shift inside herself at the thought, a letting go. It wasn't that she was any less heartbroken or angry or afraid but she had reached a limit now and was moving into something new.

State troopers had roadblocked the I-65 on-ramps, funneling all traffic north. Percy took a chance on some nameless rural route, thinking that as long as he kept heading south he'd eventually wind up in Mobile. The wind was really blowing now, making the truck veer and shudder, and the rain seemed less like itself than some diabolical invention of the wind. Every couple of miles, his headlights picked out a tree down in the road but he managed each time to creep past on the shoulder or in the other lane. Nothing out here but woods. He should have turned around hours ago but he'd sat there at the gas pump, long after the woman with the birthmark had locked the doors, unable to make himself retreat to Horseshoe Bend.

Mutt whined and scratched the window.

"Trust me," Percy said. "You don't wanna stick your head out."

He was thinking about his father all of a sudden, how he always had a dog up at the camp, always a lab, always well-bred and well trained but half-ruined by the easy life. His father liked to duck hunt and he liked a good dog to hunt with, but his expectations were minimal. If a dog wasn't gun shy, if it didn't lose too many ducks in the marsh grass, A.B. Ransom was content. He didn't care about a dog drinking from the toilet or letting itself up on the couch when the men had relinquished it for the night. He didn't care much if it chewed his ducks a little on the way back to the blind. His father bought Horseshoe Bend when Percy was three years old and he could remember going up there when Angus was still too young to tag along, just him and his father. The cold, early mornings. The dog shivering in the blind. The mist over the water and the lazy rising of the sun. The way those mornings felt reminded Percy of church. He was not, like other boys, driven to distraction by impatience during a Mass. Even very young, he had a sense, bred into him by his mother, that there was something in the world bigger than his own life. Religion promised the possibility of that mysterious something becoming clear. The problem was that the Mass never lived up to his expectations. The gospel, the homily, the ritual of communion. *Lord, I am not worthy to receive you, but only say the word and I shall be healed.* Those mornings with his father, on the other hand, they delivered without fail. Perfect quiet for hours, then the voices of the ducks, like distant laughter, then his old man whispering, "OK, boy. Easy now. Here they come." He might have been talking to Percy or the dog or to himself. It didn't matter. Then, at last, the thunder of his father's side-by-side fired in empty woods. Every time.

He couldn't have been more than thirty miles from the city limits when he came upon a flooded bridge, this nothing creek gone bigheaded with the storm surge, all stirred up, shrugging its banks, rushing over and around the bridge and into the road on either side. Percy inched forward until he could hear the exhaust pipe beginning to gurgle in the water. He stopped and pounded the wheel.

"Fuck my luck," he said.

He could make out three feet of guardrail, which meant the creek had likely risen only a foot or two higher than the bridge. The bridge itself was only forty feet across. He hadn't seen another road for half an hour and he didn't want to back-track now, not when he was so close. He reversed out of the flood, then eased back in, keeping a gentle but steady pressure on the accelerator. He felt the current right away, trying to float the truck, shoving him toward the rail, the water deeper than he'd guessed. The engine cut out on him halfway. He cursed and turned the key a few times but he knew it was no use.

"Well, Mutt," he said. Then he said, "Were you aware that the Roe River in Montana is the shortest river in the world? You should know that. That's your home state."

He opened his last beer and sat there for a minute watching the storm. The truck rocked in the current like a boat on gentle seas. The only thing

Percy could think to do was bail out and swim the creek, find a house or something on the other side, somebody who could help. He had no idea what came after that. He rolled the window down and hauled Mutt into his lap. He was trying to convince the dog to jump, when, to his surprise, the railing creaked and splintered and the current washed his back end around so he was looking upstream a moment, his rear wheels poised over nothing. Then it was like the bottom dropped out of the Earth and Percy remembered to hold his breath as he plunged into the creek, Mutt scrambling and confused, water pouring through the window, beer cans floating by his head, the whole world upside down and dark.

It wasn't as bad as Kathleen expected. Aunt Nora got them situated in the walk-in pantry and they had plenty of food in there and a portable radio, which seemed so old-timey to Kathleen, so quaint, and Aunt Nora lit a bunch of candles when the power went out, illuminating the pantry like a vigil or a honeymoon or a ghost story. She brought blankets and pillows and Murphy's bassinette and lots of extra diapers and Lucy was curious about the baby—How much did he eat? How much did he sleep? Why did they name the baby Murphy? Aunt Nora had been distracted by their arrival at first, almost irritated, Kathleen thought, but she warmed to Lucy's questions. Turned out Murphy was Aunt Nora's maiden name.

"Your grandmother wanted him to be the third," she said, whispering because the baby was asleep.

Lucy said, "The third what?"

Sometimes, her sister was so stupid, so young, that Kathleen wanted to hit her in the head, but other times her nearness to childhood charmed Kathleen and made her jealous in a way she couldn't have explained. Aunt Nora had encouraged them to eat the perishables from the fridge so Lucy was spooning ice cream straight out of the carton, smearing her chin, and Kathleen had to resist the impulse to give her a hug. "Angus Bradshaw Ransom *the third*," she said, and Lucy's eyes and mouth went perfectly round with comprehension, as if a mystery of the universe had been explained. Aunt Nora did a quiet laugh, a slumber party laugh, and dipped a spoon into a carton of her own.

"Your Uncle Percy told me the craziest thing one time," she said.

The close quarters and the forced quiet and the wavery light combined somehow to make Kathleen aware of her whole body, every muscle and bone, the follicles of her hair and the bottoms of her feet and the inside of her nose—the air in the pantry was thick with complicated smells—and this awareness of herself, of being alive at just this moment, made her think of Dexter and what they had planned and she couldn't help wondering if Dexter was thinking of her as well.

"He claimed," Aunt Nora said, "that newborns always look more like their fathers than their mothers, that there's some prehistoric strand of DNA hardwired into every species to keep fathers from eating their young."

Lucy said, "Uncle Percy is so weird."

"I wish Dad had eaten you," Kathleen said, and Lucy flicked her with her ice cream spoon, leaving a smear on Kathleen's neck. Kathleen swiped the ice cream with her finger and stuck her finger in Lucy's ear and Lucy, squealing, batted Kathleen's hand away.

Aunt Nora shushed them but it was clear she was amused.

"He probably made it up," Aunt Nora said. "You might have noticed that your Uncle Percy is more than a little full of shit."

This was true, Kathleen thought, but also one of the reasons she liked Uncle Percy, how different he was than Uncle Angus and her own parents, how little he seemed to care what they thought of him, how little he seemed to care about anything at all. She considered being offended on his behalf but decided that Aunt Nora sounded more affectionate than rude.

"He told me once that humans blink over ten million times a year."

"Why would anyone know that?" Lucy said.

Between bursts of static, the radio murmured on about the storm, volume turned down low enough that Murphy wouldn't be disturbed. "According to

the National Weather Service, Hurricane Raphael
came ashore at . . . three feet of water in Bienville
Square . . . one eyewitness reports . . ." Sometimes, when the static crackled, Murphy fidgeted
and twitched and brought his fists up to his face,
but he never woke enough to fuss. "Evacuation
of Dauphin Island . . . gusts up to 160 miles per
hour . . . emergency room closed at Mobile Infir-
mary due to . . ."

Was Kathleen worried about her mother and
her grandmother? Yes, of course, but how could
she explain the way it felt to be here with her
aunt and her baby cousin and her sister with this
hurricane beating against the house? The candle-
light, the radio. When they got bored with storm
reports, Aunt Nora twirled the dial looking for
music, found an AM station broadcasting hits
from the eighties. One particular line from a song
Kathleen had never heard before got stuck in her
head. *When love walks in the room/Everybody stand up.*
Those words kept scrolling across her mind while
she waited for Lucy and Aunt Nora to fall asleep.
Finally, the wind died down outside and she felt

a heavier silence settling over the pantry and she stepped quietly past her sister and her aunt and skirted Murphy's bassinette and slipped out the back door into the night. *When love walks in the room/ Everybody stand up.*

According to Dexter, they would have an hour or so of calm before the rest of the hurricane caught up, a hole in the fabric of the weather. She'd heard the expression before, of course, *eye of the storm*, but even so the silver moon caught her off guard, the way the sky had opened up, all those stars making their presence known inside a ring of clouds. It was exactly as beautiful as Dexter had promised. *When loves walks in the room.* Dexter was seventeen. His family lived around the block. He'd proposed their usual meeting place. Uncle Percy's lot. He'd have no trouble sneaking out. His parents were older than Kathleen's grandmother, too old to keep up with him anymore. He had a brother in his forties, bipolar, institutionalized since long before Dexter was born, and his parents hadn't meant to risk another child. *Everybody stand up.* But Dexter was perfect, those broad shoulders, the way his hair was cut too short, so tall his arms and legs went on forever.

Earlier that day, she'd swiped a cigarette from her mother's hiding place in the tampon box under the bathroom sink and she lit it now, wanted Dexter to taste it when he kissed her, smoked as she picked her way through the debris, limbs and shingles everywhere. She noticed the fallen oak almost right away but registered it out of order, as if her subconscious was protecting her from the sight, its root base first, making a lean-to over a flooded crater in the ground, then its trunk, split in two across the middle on impact, and then its upper reaches, caving in through the roof of her grandmother's house, taking the balcony and section of wall with it as it fell, the lesion V-shaped, like the house had been unzipped. At first, she could hardly believe her eyes and then she did believe and she gasped and dropped her cigarette in a puddle. *When loves walks in the room/Everybody stand up.* She could see Dexter's flashlight playing on the magnolia leaves and quickened her pace across the lawn.

"There she is," he said, as Kathleen ducked under the branches.

They kissed until she raised her arms so he could help her with her shirt.

"I've got a song stuck in my head."

"Sucks," he said.

They kissed again while Kathleen unbuckled his belt.

Dexter asked her, "How's your grandmother?"

"I don't want to talk about that," she said.

They were standing under the tree, her shirt and his pants draped on the nearest branch, the flashlight balanced on its base, its beam illuminating the upper reaches and catching on wet leaves like candle flames. The truth was she didn't know the answer to his question. Nobody's phones were working. They hadn't heard from her mother since she left. Kathleen was just about to step back into his arms when a noise separated itself from the night. She couldn't put her finger on the sound but it was somehow human and right away she knew that Lucy had followed her from the house. She crossed her arms over her chest. "What?" Dexter said. *When love walks in the room/Everybody stand up.* For what felt like a long time, she stood there looking at him, thinking Lucy had seen this much already, thinking how awful and magnificent was the world, wondering what were the chances a moment like this, exactly like this, would ever come along in her life again.

The old man was sitting in the stairwell, resting the barrel of a single-shot .410 on his bottom teeth and listening to the storm blunder around. He'd left the windows open wide. The house was a hundred years old, two over two, bedrooms up, kitchen and parlor down, and there was nothing here that mattered. The wind whipped past him on the stairs, stinging wet, surprised and angry sounding, he thought, at meeting no resistance. It had already taken his screened porch, the roof above his bedroom. He'd installed indoor plumbing twenty years ago but the bathroom was little more than a corrugated tin amendment to the kitchen and the storm had snatched that away as well.

He thought for a moment he heard a voice but that was impossible. It had to be a trick of wind. In the cedars. In the soybeans. In the kitchen.

In addition to the shotgun, he had a flashlight and a pint of Early Times with him on the stairs. He heard the voice again, was able to make out the word, "Anybody——" before the wind tore it to shreds. He slipped the barrel from his mouth and spat to clear the taste. He never had visitors. No way was somebody in the house on a night like this but he pushed to his feet anyhow, peeked around the corner. A shadow, a flicker of darkness deeper than the night. He stepped down off the stairs, gripped the unlit flashlight in his left hand and braced the .410 on his hip.

"What the hell?" he said, and hit the light.

There before him was the figure of a man, shirt-less, barefoot, slicked brown with mud, his hair all wild angles from his head, arms covering his face like he'd never been exposed to artificial light. He might have shot. He would have been within his rights. But he only had one shell and it was spoken for. The figure was lowering his hands, patting the air between them, speaking now, his voice drowned out by wind. The old man waved with the shotgun, indicating the stairs. He walked the figure halfway up, used the .410 to let him know that he should sit.

"Talk," he said.

The figure said, "I lost my dog."

"I used to have a dog."

"My truck is in the creek," the figure said.

"Used to have one of those, too," the old man said. "Now I just take the tractor when I need to go to town."

The story that the figure told, shouting to be heard over the storm, took longer than the old man expected but it was just wild and dark enough to be believed. He spoke of mothers and hospitals, a washed-out bridge. He backed up in time and came forward again, crying now, partly, the old man thought, because of what he'd been through on this night but also because of the story he was telling. Some of what he said was lost to wind. Even more came out a jumbled mess. But the old man heard enough. The impossibility of living up to the past. The burden of trying. A last chance to measure up. Finally, the story caught up to the present, the house in the field, maybe a mile from the swollen creek, the two men here upon the stairs, one young, one old, both beset by storm.

The old man fished in his pocket for a key.

"Do you know how to drive a tractor?" he said.

The figure stared at the key the old man dropped into his palm like it was precious and strange.

"I'll buy you a new tractor. I'll buy you a new truck, too. What's your number? I'll call as soon as I can."

"No phone," the old man said.

"Then your address?"

"Don't matter," the old man said. "No way you're gonna make it."

He laughed and sipped the Early Times.

"I have to make it," the figure said.

He used the key to scratch his phone number into the drywall. The old man followed him down the stairs and they stepped through an open window into the storm. The old man went no farther than what was left of his front porch, had to cling to a post to keep upright in the wind. He watched the figure crab low across the ground to the tractor, watched the tractor receding down the drive, one taillight busted out, the other a dying red pinprick in the fabric of this enormous night.

When the tractor was out of sight, he returned to the stairs and put the barrel of the .410 back in his mouth. The hurricane didn't pay him any mind. After a minute, he took the barrel out and leaned the shotgun against the wall. He had to admit that he was curious. He couldn't remember being curious about much of anything in a long, long time. He decided to wait, maybe give it a day or two. Then, if the hurricane saw fit to spare him, he'd hitchhike to town and call the number on his wall and find out if his tractor had brought this stranger safely through the storm.

Angus carried the cage back through the holds, sealing everything shut behind him, the bird quiet after all that talk. Morris was radioing their position to the Coast Guard when he returned.

Standard procedure in these conditions. Call in every couple of hours so somebody would know where to start looking if they went down. Wind and rain lashing the wheelhouse, waves swamping the bow, Bullard leaning into the wheel with his legs apart, his cap turned backward on his head.

Morris signed off with the Coast Guard. Over his shoulder, without looking, he said, "We were about to flip a coin to see which one of us would have to break it to your wife."

"I found this bird," Angus said.

Morris stiffened. Angus saw it in his shoulders, his neck.

"That's Dinah," he said. "That's my bird." He turned to Angus, then, his expression difficult to read. "I live out on Dauphin Island. Maybe you knew that. I couldn't leave them all."

"How many do you have?" Angus said.

"Sixteen," Morris said. "Different kinds."

Angus pictured exotic birds perched on the backs of chairs like doves perched on a power line, Morris's life unbidden before his eyes, molted feathers, cages, seed, newspaper, a charcoal grill where Morris did most of his cooking because it was too hard to keep the kitchen clean. Angus could see the storm surge sweeping under the house, wind shattering in through the windows, all those birds whipped to death like doomed confetti.

"What kind is Dinah?"

"She's a mynah bird."

"Dinah the mynah?"

"That's right," Morris said.

Angus passed him the cage and Morris scanned around for a place to put it, settled on the captain's chair. He instructed Angus to take the wheel, sent Bullard below deck to hunt for rope. He pushed a finger through the bars. The bird nipped him with its beak but said nothing, as if it understood that it had revealed a secret in its terror and was ashamed. *I'm so alone.* His father would have let Morris keep his pride.

"Thank you," he said.

Morris said, "For what?"

"For being here. For getting us this far."

Morris made a face. "Thank the boat," he said.

Bullard clattered back up the stairs a minute later bearing a length of rope. While Morris secured the cage, Angus tried to return the wheel to Bullard but Bullard said, "You take her," and the *Kagero* plowed down the backside of a swell. Angus felt the wheel jumping and fighting in his hands but he held her steady through the trough, bow lights glimmering and bobbing in the rain. Took a moment to realize that he was seeing bow lights at all, the world no longer blotted out by the whiteness of the storm, and it dawned on him that his seasickness had passed. He thought of his wife, his son. Checked his bearings. Tried to sort out how many more hours before they might begin the slow turn back toward Mobile, but he couldn't make the numbers line up in his head.

"You know what the name means?" he said.

"What name?" Bullard said.

"*Kagero.*"

They stood there looking at him.

"It means 'the shimmering mist that rises from the earth on a hot day.'"

"No shit?" Morris said.

"No shit," Angus said.

Muriel didn't know what time it was when A.B. came up to bed. To her surprise, she'd drifted off and now the mattress shifted and she opened her eyes and there he was, slump-backed, rubbing his face with both hands. She could hear the clock ticking on the nightstand but couldn't turn to look because she was covered up with sleeping children, Doodle on one side, Angus on the other, Percy draped across her lap.

"Everything all right?" she whispered.

A.B. smiled over his shoulder, tired, unconvincing.

"I called his father. I didn't want to get the police."

How on earth had she managed to fall asleep on the heels of such a fright?

"They've been through enough," she said.

He stood without reply and began to undress, peeling his shirt over his arms, revealing his broad shoulders, tufts of hair springing up around the collar of his undershirt. Her husband had a country boy's physique, she thought, big and round, soft-looking but strong, his power an afterthought, innate rather than cultivated.

"I might have killed that boy," he said.

He removed his dentures, dropped them in a glass of water, then dropped in one of the cleaning tablets, which made a sizzling noise like whispers. He stared into the glass as if he was reflected in it. After a moment, he clapped a hand over his mouth and began to cry. He didn't make a sound. You wouldn't have known to look at him but she could tell. She understood her husband well enough to be certain that his tears were born not only of what might have happened on this night but of the fact that no matter how strong he was, he didn't have it in him to ward off all the danger and tragedy in the world, not even from his family. She knew as well that if she spoke, he'd push her away. So she watched him cry in silence. It didn't last long. He wiped his eyes, his nose. He braced his hands on the chest of drawers and breathed until he was himself again.

"I love you," she said.

"You look so comfortable," he said. "I'll sleep in Percy's bed."

"No."

"There's not enough room for me."

"There is," she said.

She rearranged her legs and A.B. stretched out atop the covers at her feet, his back to her, knees drawn up like a little boy. They were quiet for a while, nothing to hear but the children drawing breath and the grandfather clock at the bottom of the stairs ticking faintly, steadily toward the hour. Finally, her husband began to speak. He told her what had happened in the kitchen after she left and they rehashed those awful minutes before they knew how the night would end. It was, in its way, the story of their life together. The comfort she took in his presence, the comfort he took in hers. His voice lulled her drowsy and she let her eyes drift shut, felt lifted out of herself somehow, rising, dreaming, rising, saw what she believed was a strange and powerful vision of the future. *Holy Mary, Mother of God, pray for us sinners, now and at the hour of our death.* She saw a dog sniffing the air for the scent that would lead him home. She saw a girl she'd never seen before tangled up with a pale-skinned boy, a second girl filled up with wonder at the sight. She saw a woman sleeping with a baby in the dark. She saw her house, this house, rent asunder, which nearly made her gasp, but then she saw her children all grown up and beautiful and in motion, Angus by sea, Percy by land, Doodle climbing a flight of stairs. There was darkness in the vision, the tumult of a storm, but such was life and she took heart in the fact that her children were drawing closer to her rather than away.

acknowledgments

Thanks to my agent, Warren Frazier, and to my editor at Grove Atlantic, Elisabeth Schmitz, two excellent friends who have been in my writing life for so long now I'm not sure I would know how to proceed without them. Thanks to everyone at Grove Atlantic, especially Katie Raissian, Deb Seager, and Julia Berner-Tobin, for all their hard work on this book. Thanks to Morgan Entrekin for his continuing faith in my fiction. Thanks to Jim McLaughlin, impossibly generous and long-suffering first reader. Thanks to Shannon Burke, Margaret Lazarus Dean, and Chris Hebert, all of whom read very early, very different versions of this collection. A special thank-you to Allen

Wier, the most thoughtful close reader I have ever known. Many thanks to the journal editors whose insight and support helped these stories become their best and final selves—Emily Nemens, Ladette Randolph, Peter Ho Davies, M. M. M. Hayes, Aaron Alford, and Adam Ross. Every word of fiction that I've ever written has been shaped by other, more talented writers in one way or another. For some reason, I've always resisted the impulse to thank them by name, though I have often been tempted to do just that. In the case of *Evening-land*, some of my favorite writers are directly referenced in these pages, others alluded to in purely personal ways, still others visible in the fingerprints of their influence, and I want to thank them here. Thank you, Walker Percy. Thank you, F. Scott Fitzgerald. Thank you, Flannery O'Connor. Thank you, James Salter. Thank you, John Cheever. Thank you, Alice Munro. Thank you, Peter Taylor. Thank you, Donald Barthelme. Thank you, Sherwood Anderson. And of course, thanks to my wife, Jill, and my daughters, Mary and Helen, for their patience and understanding and for providing an endless array of distractions from the inside of my head. Finally, thanks to my colleagues and students at the University of Tennessee—there are too many to name—for making it such a pleasure to come to work. Thank you all.